Search for Treasure

"This is storytelling for young readers at its finest—equal parts summer adventure and environmental suspense, *The Islanders* is a middle-grade love letter to family, friendship, and the natural world." —Kwame Alexander, *New York Times* bestselling and Newbery Medal-winning author of *The Crossover*

"A tender, warmhearted tale in a memorable setting." — *Kirkus Reviews*

"Monroe and May's middle-grade debut is a thoroughly wholesome adventure." —*School Library Journal*

"The small-town community instills a strong sense of place, and the trio's chemistry holds promise for future installments." —*Publishers Weekly*

Also by
Mary Alice Monroe with Angela May

The Islanders

Mary Alice Monroe

with Angela May

The Islanders

SEARCH FOR TREASURE

ALADDIN
NEW YORK LONDON TORONTO SYDNEY NEW DELHI

ALADDIN

An imprint of Simon & Schuster Children's Publishing Division
1230 Avenue of the Americas, New York, New York 10020
First Aladdin hardcover edition June 2022
Text copyright © 2022 by Mary Alice Monroe
Jacket illustrations copyright © 2022 by Jennifer Bricking
Interior illustrations copyright © 2022 by Jennifer Bricking
All rights reserved, including the right of reproduction in whole or in part in any form.
ALADDIN and related logo are registered trademarks of Simon & Schuster, Inc.
For information about special discounts for bulk purchases, please contact Simon & Schuster Special Sales at 1-866-506-1949 or business@simonandschuster.com.
The Simon & Schuster Speakers Bureau can bring authors to your live event. For more information or to book an event contact the Simon & Schuster Speakers Bureau at 1-866-248-3049 or visit our website at www.simonspeakers.com.
Designed by Tiara Iandiorio
The text of this book was set in Adobe Caslon Pro.
Manufactured in the United States of America 0422 FFG
10 9 8 7 6 5 4 3 2 1
This book has been cataloged with the Library of Congress.
ISBN 978-1-5344-2730-3 (hc)
ISBN 978-1-5344-2731-0 (pbk)
ISBN 978-1-5344-2732-7 (eBook)

We dedicated *The Islanders* to our children and grandchildren.
This book is dedicated to our husbands:
Markus John Potter Kruesi
Charles Jaeson May.
May you always remain young at heart.

CHAPTER 1

Back to Dewees Island

THIS WAS GOING TO BE THE BEST SUMMER ever!

I stood at the bow of the ferry plowing along the Intracoastal Waterway. My hands clutched the ferry railing as the salt-scented sea air cut through my hair. I was on my way back to Dewees Island! My heart raced as fast as the big boat engines below, whipping the water into a frothy wake.

To my right I spotted a small motorboat gaining on the double-decker ferry. I hurried to the side, and shading my eyes from the sun's glare, I squinted and saw a girl with a long blond braid driving the boat. My mouth dropped open.

"Lovie!" I shouted, and waved my arm overhead.

The girl turned and tooted the boat's horn. Then, with a smile, she gunned the engine. I laughed out loud as she sped past the ferry and soon became a small dot in the distance. Lovie only had one speed—fast.

Seeing her buzz by in her boat, I couldn't wait to get out on a motorboat again, to feel the wind push back my hair, or kayak on a lazy, slow-moving creek, or swim in the wild waves of the ocean, feeling the sun on my face. I couldn't wait to do my chores in the golf cart! Most of all, I couldn't wait to see my friends.

We had all promised to stay in touch during the school year, but it was hard when you lived in different cities and had different schedules. When I did try to text them, I didn't know what to say. It felt so awkward. Macon and I did meet up online sometimes to battle together in our favorite video games. But when Lovie sent a text—which wasn't often—our messages went like this:

Lovie: Hi!

Me: Hi

Lovie: How was school? My day was B O R I N G

Me: Yeah. Same.

Lovie: Ok. TTYL

But still, I missed them. And I wouldn't have to wait long to see my friends in real life!

The ferry slowed in the No Wake zone as the trees grew larger and the dock drew closer on Dewees Island. A cluster of people stood waiting at the dock. It was easy to spot Fire Chief Rand towering over everyone else with his broad shoulders and red hair. Next to him, my grandmother, Honey, looked tiny. Her white hair was longer, pulled back in a ponytail. They were holding up a large sign with bright red letters: WELCOME HOME ERIC AND JAKE!

Then I saw my fellow Islanders—Macon and Lovie—waving madly, jumping up and down and calling out "Jaaaaaaake!"

I spun around and raced down the stairs from the top deck, my feet rattling the metal stairs. I stopped abruptly at the door and scoped out the main cabin through the foggy window. A woman sat with her small dog in her lap. Two construction workers were looking at their phones. An elderly couple sat talking in low voices. My gaze zeroed in on my dad. He sat on the bench with his shoulders ramrod straight in military style and looked out the window. His good leg was bent at the knee, but his prosthesis was stretched straight out in front of him. You couldn't tell the leg was artificial by looking at it under his pants, but I knew. "Prosthesis" is a big name, but my dad said it's just a fancy name for a fake leg. I looked at his hands. They lay flat on his thighs, but his fingers were tapping. That was my clue he was nervous. I took a breath and pushed open the door.

"Hey, Dad, everyone's here to greet us!" I shouted as I ran up to him. "They even made a sign."

My dog, Lucky, leaped to his feet at seeing me. His tail wagged, he panted, and his eyes were bright. I could always count on Lucky for excitement.

Just like I could count on my dad for being sad. Mom said he was trying really hard and that we had to encourage him. And I do. The pressure at home was one of the reasons I was super glad to be going back to Dewees, where I could just hang out with my best friends.

"Yeah, I see them," Dad said, turning from the window, then pushed out a smile. "Looks like your friends can't wait to see you again."

"And your friend, too," I replied, trying to make him feel as excited as I was. Fire Chief Rand and my dad had been friends on Dewees since they were kids.

As the boat eased into position at the dock, the other passengers all rose at once and began collecting their bags. I knew my dad would wait until the boat stopped rocking and everyone else had left before he stood up. He didn't like having anyone behind, rushing him.

I walked on one side of my dad as he made his way off the boat, pausing at the six inches of air space between the edge of the dock and the rocking boat. Sometimes, something small can feel very big.

"Need some help?" the mate asked.

I cringed. My dad hated to be asked if he needed help.

Suddenly Lucky leaped with joy across to the dock with ease. He stood on the dock and looked back at us, tail wagging, like he was saying, *It's easy! What are you waiting for?*

Dad chuckled and shook his head. "Nope, thanks." He boldly stepped across the opening.

I paused and thought to myself, *I'm back.* From the moment I stepped off the boat, I felt I was in another world. The noise faded away. No sounds of city life. Instead of packed neighborhoods, congested roads, and busy shops, I saw trees, acres of green cordgrass, and water everywhere. It felt like all my worries were whooshing out with the deep breath I released, like a balloon fizzing out.

I gave Lucky a pat, and we followed Dad down the wooden dock. Dad kept his shoulders straight and walked at a good pace, but he had a tilted gait. Not a limp as much as a sway when he favored the left leg. I wanted to run but stayed with him.

When we made it to the end of the dock, everyone was clapping and laughing. Honey was even crying. It was only the beginning of June, and already Honey was so tan it made her blue eyes shine like the sky above. They were the same blue as my dad's, except hers seemed to sparkle like the water around us. Honey began hugging me so tight I could barely breathe.

"Dear boy, I was counting the days, and now you're here," she exclaimed.

I pretended to compare my height to hers, moving my hand from the top of my head to over her head. "This year, I'm definitely taller than you." How tall I was getting was always the icebreaker between us when she visited our house.

"And so you are," she replied, stepping back and letting her eyes sweep over me like a scanner cataloging every change. I did the same. Honey had lost some weight in a good way and seemed more fit in her usual khaki shorts and Turtle Team T-shirt.

Honey shook her head with a rueful smile. "You're getting taller and I'm getting shorter. That's the way it works." She grinned ear to ear. "I just can't believe I have my best boys together for the summer!"

With that, she turned to my dad, opening her arms to him. I stepped aside. Dad was her only child, and she doted on him. Honey had a hard time when he was injured last year, especially so soon after she lost my grandpa.

Suddenly arms grabbed me and squeezed so tight I could barely speak.

"What took you so long, bro?" Macon asked as he released me.

Talk about getting taller! I looked up at my friend, and I mean *up*. Macon had grown maybe four inches since last summer. And what was that growing over his lip?

"Dude," I said, pointing to his lip at a line of black fuzz. "Is that a mustache?"

Macon shrugged and self-consciously wiped his hand across his mouth. "It's nothing."

"You could say that again," Lovie said with a laugh. "Now, my turn!" She lunged forward to deliver a hug. Then she reached over to wrap one arm around Macon in a group hug. "This is so awesome to all be together again!"

"Personal space," Macon said, trying to gently wiggle free.

Lovie's face flamed, and she dropped her arms and bent to hug Lucky, who was super happy for anyone's attention.

Lovie had changed, too, since last summer, but I wasn't exactly sure how. Her long yellow braid was the same, and her eyes were still as blue as the ocean on a sunny day. Maybe she was taller. And her brown freckles seemed brighter than I remembered. Something was making her look older. She glanced up at me, flashing her bright smile. My cheeks burned, and I felt awkward not knowing what to say.

Thankfully, I heard Honey calling my name. I turned to see the grown-ups gathering our luggage and heading toward the long line of golf carts parked beside the wooden boardwalk.

No cars were allowed on Dewees. Or stores. This island was a nature sanctuary, and the people living here took care to protect it. No one more than my grandmother. She was one of the very first to move onto the island and took every opportunity to remind folks of that. I saw her walking toward the shabbiest-looking golf cart in the row. A Turtle Team sticker dominated the left corner of the windshield.

"Let's all stop off at the Nature Center first," Honey exclaimed. "I have a little party set out. Nothing much, just some cake and soda. I'm so glad you're finally here, and I want to show y'all what I've done to the place." She spoke to all of us, but her eyes were on my dad.

"You go on. I'm, uh, not ready for parties yet. I'll head to the house, if you don't mind," Dad said. "I'll get settled in."

I winced. My dad didn't like parties or attending events ever since the war, and I could tell by his tense smile that he was uncomfortable being away from home. It was as though every new place he went was a series of tests he had to endure.

Honey's smile fell, but she hoisted it back in place. "Oh ... of course. I can show you the Rec Center later."

Chief Rand plopped my duffel bag into the golf cart. "Y'all go ahead," he boomed in a cheery voice. "I'll take Eric to the house. It'll give us a chance to catch up. We'll take my cart."

"I'll save you both some cake . . . ," Honey offered.

"All right. See you guys later," Dad said, and turned to walk toward Chief Rand's cart. He met my gaze. "See you later, son."

Macon, Lovie, and I exchanged glances. I narrowed my eyes as I watched Honey head toward her golf cart without another word.

Macon stepped closer and said in a low voice, "Hey, how's your dad doing?"

I shrugged, feeling my defenses going up even with my best friend. "Oh, he's okay. He just gets tired easily."

"Let's go to the Nature Center," Lovie said, bringing cheer back to the conversation. "You've got to meet Pierre."

Pierre stared back at me from his large tank. The diamondback terrapin stood on his hind legs, his front legs clawing at the glass. He looked to be the size of my hand, with a brown shell and gray speckled skin.

"Look closer," Lovie said, by my side. "See the black line along his beak?" She giggled.

"Hey, he has a mustache," I said, turning to look at Macon. "Just like you!"

"Ha, ha. Very funny," Macon replied, putting his nose up to the turtle tank for a better look. "The sign on his tank says they are the only turtle species to live their entire life in the salt marsh." Macon straightened. "That's a cool fact."

"You should feed this guy," I told Honey. "He acts like he's starving."

"Oh, he's just being Pierre," Honey said with a wave of her hand as she walked closer. "I just fed him a few periwinkles and insects. He always bangs on the glass like that. He just likes the attention."

Lovie looked up. "I thought turtles didn't like to be held."

"They don't," Honey agreed. "They prefer to be left alone, like Shelley over there." She guided us to a separate aquarium, where another turtle, all brown, sat on a rock, her nose to the corner. It looked like she wanted to stay far away from us . . . and Pierre. "Pierre has a crush on Shelley, but she's a mud turtle and wants nothing to do with him. She snaps at him if he gets too friendly." Honey sighed dramatically. "Our Pierre is just a lover."

"Oh, that's so sad," Lovie said, and bent to look closer at the turtle. "I'll be your friend."

I gazed around the Nature Center. It felt fresh and new, with posters of local animals and birds and several shelves of books all neatly categorized. There was even a section for Dewees Island T-shirts, ball caps, and mugs. Next to the merchandise display hung a big cork board decorated with a summer activities calendar and a local news section. On it were pinned newspaper clippings and photos of Dewees residents out and about doing island things. What caught my eye was the front of the *Post and Courier* newspaper tacked dead center to the board. The headline read:

LOCAL TREASURE HUNTER FINDS GOLD COIN ON DEWEES ISLAND

Beneath the headline was a close-up photo of an old man's wrinkled hands holding a dark, dirty coin with specks of gold shining through the grime and sand. Not taking my eyes off the article, I hollered for my friends.

"Hey, guys! Check this out!"

Lovie and Macon leaned in to see what I was reading.

"A gold doubloon!" Macon yelled as he started unpinning the newspaper clipping from the board. He read sections out loud.

> Harold Maynard, a resident of Dewees Island, walks the beach daily with his metal detector, hunting for lost items in the sand. Today he made a rare find buried slightly beneath the sand: a gold coin the Vietnam War veteran believes was unearthed by the storm system that pounded the coastline this week. Local historians said Maynard's find could be a coin long buried by the famous

pirate Blackbeard. Maynard said, "I like to believe there's a lot more treasure hidden out here on this little island. I won't stop looking, either."

"So, you found out about Mr. Maynard's discovery?" Honey said, walking closer. "That's been the talk of the island."

"When did he find it?" asked Macon.

"Take a look at the date on the article," she replied. "Get the facts, children."

"April twenty-sixth," said Lovie, her nose close to the newspaper clipping. She turned to face us, eyes wide. "That was just five weeks ago."

We all looked at one another in silent amazement for a few seconds. Then an idea burst out of me.

"We've got to find that treasure!"

Pierre →

CHAPTER 2

Nature makes children of us all

SEVERAL GATORS LAZILY SUNNED ON THE bank at the far side of the pond as Honey and I cruised along the road to the Bird's Nest, Honey's house. I was back behind the wheel of our golf cart, and it all came back to me, just like riding a bicycle.

Next to me, Honey balanced a plate of leftover cake on her lap. I slowly turned off the road where the small wooden sign read THE POTTERS, DEWEES ISLAND, SC. When I left last summer, her driveway had been cleared of debris, but it was overgrown again. Overgrown grasses and palmetto fronds scraped the cart as I plowed through the morass. Living on a wild island, things grow wild!

The Bird's Nest got its name because it stood high on wooden pilings to nestle up in the trees. Sun rays cut through the tall branches and dappled the house. I breathed in the salt-scented air and smiled. I'd come home. I knew this place. I loved it. I felt safe here.

I'd be lying if I didn't admit it'd been a tough year since I left Dewees. We moved to nearby Mount Pleasant from New Jersey with high hopes because Mom got a new assignment flying those huge C-17 cargo planes in the Air Force. And being closer to Honey was great for the family.

Only we never visited Dewees Island in the past year. Not once.

Honey came to visit us in Mount Pleasant because Dad couldn't climb all the stairs of the Bird's Nest. My new school was okay. I made a couple of friends, but they were just kids I hung out with *at* school. I didn't invite anyone over to hang out at my house.

Living with Dad was like walking on eggshells. Mom kept telling me to be patient, that he had a lot of changes to get used to, like being medically discharged from the Army. And losing his leg. And dealing with the death of his friends.

Yeah, those were really big things. But we were *all* getting used to those changes.

"Park to the right of that cart, Jake," Honey said, pointing to a spiffy new golf cart.

"Nice and easy," I replied, using Honey's words from the time she taught me how to drive a golf cart. I eased like a pro into the spot right next to the other cart. This cart was a shiny moss-green color with clean, rugged tires. Parking next to it made Honey's old golf cart look even worse.

"Whose golf cart is that?" I asked, hopping out to inspect it.

Her eyes gleamed with pride as she put her hands on her hips. "It's a surprise for your dad. I thought he'd enjoy it. It's what they call 'street-worthy,' with power steering, seat belt, and a few adjustments he needs for . . . well, you know."

I knew she meant my dad's prosthetic leg. Why didn't she just say the word? It's like everyone avoided what we all could see right in front of us.

"So now you own the oldest and the newest golf carts on the island?" I teased her.

Honey laughed and, putting her hands on my shoulders, turned me to face the old golf cart. "And that means this cart is officially yours now."

My mouth fell open. "You mean, like, it's *mine?*"

"All yours. Take good care of it." She lifted one brow. "And remember the island rules."

"Yes, ma'am," I replied with a wide grin. I remembered my first cart ride with Honey last summer, when she taught me how to drive. The safety rules included a warning about Big Al, the biggest, baddest, most respected alligator on Dewees.

"Come along, Jake. I've got a few more things to show you. This old bird has been feathering her nest." Honey pointed to the back corner of the house, where a large metal box contraption stood. There was a glowing silver button on a wall next to it.

"An elevator!"

"Sort of. It's called a lift. I got it installed so your dad can get up to the house without the worry of all the stairs here."

This meant that we'd be able to come to Dewees more often. Smiling ear to ear, I walked closer for a better look. "Sweet! Let's go on up!" I said, reaching out to press the silver button.

"Oh, no," Honey said, pushing away my hand with one swoop. "You are an able-bodied twelve-year-old. You can take the stairs. It's good for you."

"Just once?" I moaned.

"Someday. But," she said, opening the metal gate and stepping into the lift, "I find I like taking the ride, too. And there's only room for one." With a gleam in her eye, she said, "Race you up!" She pushed the button.

I heard the grinding gears of the lift and spun on my heel toward the steps, and ran up the two flights to the front door. I bent at my knees, winded but glad because the lift was slower than a turtle. As I waited for Honey, I looked around the front porch and saw colorful wildflowers spilling over the sides of the wooden containers. So different from last year when the planters only had sprigs of green weeds and dead brown plants.

"What took you so long?" I asked with a laugh when Honey stepped from the lift.

She ruffled my hair and opened the blue front door. I stepped in and was hit with a delicious smell. Dad and Chief

Rand were sitting on the sofa talking. Dad was smiling.

"Hey, Dad!" I called out. Lucky quickly jumped up, his paws slipping on the shiny wood floor as he hightailed it to my side. "Hey, boy!" I said, bending down to scruff his face and let him nuzzle my neck.

I straightened and let my gaze glide across Honey's house. Large windows encircled the house, and I blinked in the brilliant sunlight as I took in all the changes. It was the same house, but so different. All the dusty piles of books that had been scattered haphazardly last summer were neatly stored in new wooden bookcases. Her big, cushy sofa had a new tan slipcover and lots of colorful pillows. Honey's ratty old recliner was gone, too. In its place was a big leather recliner.

"Wow," I said with wonder, turning around with wide eyes. Then a thought hit me. I headed for the fridge. I grabbed the handle, then paused, flashing back to the previous summer when I found plastic containers filled with mystery meats, moldy cheese, and sour smells. I held my breath and pulled open the door.

"Wow . . . ," I whispered again. Clear containers of fresh fruit and vegetables were neatly stacked on the glistening shelves, just like Macon's mom had in her fridge. There were applesauce cups, yogurts, cheese sticks, and . . . I couldn't believe it. Cokes in glass bottles! The ultimate treat.

"Hey, Honey! You've really got this fridge stocked!"

"Yes, sir," she replied, coming closer and looking pleased that I noticed. "Want a soda?"

This was definitely a change from the start of last summer. "Yes, please."

"I thought I'd celebrate your island return with a little shrimp and grits tonight." She lifted the lid off a pot on the stove to stir the grits. "I caught the shrimp early this morning."

"*You* caught them?" I asked, trying to imagine Honey tossing out a cast net.

My dad turned my way from the sofa. "Your grandmother can harvest, hook, or catch anything Mother Nature offers." He looked over at her and his gaze held pride. "Mama, let me peel the shrimp for you."

"You sit back down. Today you're my guests. Let me fuss over the food. Don't you worry. I've got chores enough waiting for you tomorrow." As she spoke, she walked over to the sink and lifted out a bowl. "Besides, I've already got them prepped to cook."

"I best get going then, so y'all can enjoy your meal," Chief Rand said, rising to stand.

"You should stay. I've got enough for four," Honey offered. "I've cooked many a meal for you over the years."

"I do remember. But I've got some paperwork to finish up at the fire station. Thank you for the offer, Mrs. Potter," he replied. "I'll belly up to the table another time." He gave her a quick hug goodbye before heading out the door.

Honey lowered the shrimp into a pan of sautéed onions and bacon. "These shrimp take just a few minutes, so you go wash up, hear?"

"Yes, ma'am." On my way to the bathroom, I stopped dead in my tracks when I spotted a laptop and a Wi-Fi router on a small desk off the hall. I couldn't believe it! I shouted as I ran back to the kitchen, "Honey! When did you get Internet here? And a computer?"

"I'm old, but I'm not deaf!" Honey dried her hands on a towel and came closer, her eyes sparkling. She opened the laptop with pride. "I was wondering how long it'd take you to spot it."

Across the room, Dad was watching, chuckling at my response.

"But, Honey," I sputtered. "I thought you didn't ever want the Internet in your house. When did you get it? Why didn't you tell us? I thought you didn't believe in it?"

"One question at a time, child," Honey said, holding up her hands in mock defense. "First of all, I *believe* in the Internet. What kind of notion is that? I always knew it's a part of daily life for families and businesses. That was never it. I was just reluctant to have it here, in my home. It didn't feel right here on Dewees. And I admit, I was a bit of a snob about it. Still," she added, fire returning to her voice, "I think people are online too much, especially you kids."

Dad interjected. "I've got to admit, Mom, I'm as surprised as Jake. What changed your mind?"

A small smile played at her lips. "Working at the Nature Center. It's a right handy tool to order books and supplies, and when I want to do research. I still go to my books, of course," she added with import. "But it's awfully quick, I'll give it that." Honey carefully poured the cooked shrimp from the pot into a strainer bowl in the sink.

"What's your Wi-Fi name and password?" I asked, pulling my cell phone out of my pants pocket.

"Now, hold your horses there, mister," Honey replied. "I guess this is as good a time as any to talk about all this." She moved her arm to indicate the table, all set with cloth napkins and candles. "Why don't we all sit down and I'll serve dinner. Everything is ready and"—she turned to me—"I thought I heard your belly rumbling,"

In short order, Honey served us heaping helpings of shrimp and grits, and she was right. I was starving. I dove in. The shrimp was as sweet as I'd ever tasted, but I couldn't wait to find out more about the Internet here at the house. I still couldn't believe it. That was a game changer.

"I can use the computer this summer, right?" I asked, going back to the topic.

Honey waited until she'd finished chewing, took a sip of water, and dabbed her lips with a napkin. "Just because I have Internet access does not mean we're going to be online all hours of the day."

I heard the resistance in her voice. "Oh, yeah, sure," I said to reassure her.

She looked at me with her *no fooling* expression.

"Yes, we now have a computer in the house. But no, it doesn't mean everything is going to change around here. I see the value in having it. But it will not run our lives, hear? We will limit how many hours we will use it. And only certain uses are permitted. I don't want to ruin the life we have here. We need the quiet that lets the wild into our hearts and our souls. That quiet, when we can hear our thoughts, is when God comes in." She paused. "Do you understand?"

I thought all that talk about God was grown-up stuff. When I was alone outdoors, or lying in my bed in my loft, I did a lot of thinking. It helped me figure out what was important. What I wanted and what I didn't want. What I needed. If that's what she meant by God talking to me, then I got that.

"Yes, ma'am. I think so."

"Nicely said, Mom." Dad raised his glass in a toast.

Honey smiled. Looking at my empty plate, she said, "Go help yourself to seconds. And get your father some while you're up."

I hurried back from the stove with our plates, brimming with steaming shrimp and creamy grits. Sitting, I went back to the topic. "Can I bring my gaming system over?"

Honey sat straight in her chair. "Absolutely not. Never. Not ever," she said, folding her arms in front of her chest. "I swear, give an inch and they take a mile," she said to my dad.

He only shrugged and gave me a look that said, *Sorry, buddy*.

"Okay, I won't." I worried I'd be booted from the Internet before I even had a chance to log on. "I promise."

"The wild outside this house is better than any video game," Honey said with a huff.

"But what about when it rains?"

"You can read."

"You're not lacking in books around here," Dad added. "It's like they multiply while you sleep, Mom."

We all laughed because it felt like the truth.

Honey said, "This is new for me, and we just have to find a balance. I'm sure we will. We don't want to spend so much time on the computer that we lose time outdoors, being creative, or reading books. Jake," she said, turning to me and narrowing her brows. She stood up and gathered our now-empty bowls, then paused to say, "The Wi-Fi password is taped to the side of the router."

I washed the dishes while Dad wiped down the table and countertop. *The chef doesn't do dish*es was an old rule at our house.

"All right, men," Honey called out from the living room. "I have something I want to present to you." She waved her hands. "Come take a seat."

Dad and I sat on the sofa, and Honey stood in front of us. She clasped her hands. "Let's talk about our summer routine. You know the drill. Same chores as last summer. Jake, you're still in charge of taking out the trash, collecting the mail, and filling up the water jugs as needed. You were very reliable, I must say."

I grinned, and my dad reached over to pat my shoulder.

"Eric," she said, turning to my dad, "you're in charge of making sure everything works around here—the golf carts, appliances, air-conditioning. You're a pretty good handyman, if I recollect."

Now it was my turn to beam at my dad.

Honey bent to pick up two black-and-white composition notebooks from the coffee table. I recognized them as the same kind she gave me last summer. She handed one to me and one to Dad. "Your new nature journals!"

"Cool," I said, pleased. I was proud of the journal I'd created last summer.

My dad looked at his with confusion. "Thanks." He lifted the notebook, as though testing its weight. His smile was rueful. "But I'm hardly a kid anymore, Mom."

"You're never too old to journal! And it's something you can share with Jake. Besides, I wouldn't want to leave you out of the fun." Honey smiled. "Nature makes children of us all."

That evening, I climbed up the wooden ship–style ladder to my room. It was my favorite place in the entire house. It was a loft, which means instead of a fourth wall, there was the ladder and a big wooden railing that I could lean against and see the entire floor below. Like on a ship.

Above the twin bed was what I called the Heidi window, a large round window just like the one in the classic novel. Instead of Heidi's mountains, however, I looked out at a maritime forest filled with live oaks, palmettos, and pine trees. And beyond, glimpses of the mysterious marsh and winding creek. The sky was turning shades of deep blue and purple, with streaks of magenta and orange. The sign of the final minutes of daylight of my first day back on Dewees Island.

This room had been my dad's growing up. It was still filled with his things. And it was now mine. I unpacked my duffel bag, laying claim to the space. After I put my clothes into the painted wooden dresser, I went to the bookshelves and let my fingertips glide over the rows of well-read books. They'd all been my dad's, and last summer I'd read a lot of them.

And then there were the journals. Last summer Honey gave me a composition notebook, and I'd torn pages from it and written letters to my dad when he was at the hospital. He'd saved them all and had them bound into a leather journal, like the one he'd has as a kid. Now my own leather-bound journal sat next to my dad's.

I laughed, thinking of Dad's face when Honey told us we both had to create new journals this summer. I'm glad she did that. I liked the idea of doing something together this summer. Dad and I had spent a lot of time around each other this past school year. But I couldn't remember doing anything fun with him. What did Honey say tonight? *Nature makes children of us all.*

Later, when I lay in my bed, my hands under my head, I yawned, feeling the fullness of the day. My eyes blinked heavily as I stared out my large, round window. This was one of my favorite times. When the sky was dark and I could stare out the window way high into the sky to see what stage the moon was in, or if there were stars out, or if clouds were moving in.

When I'd returned to the island, I'd thought I wanted everything to be exactly the same as I left it last August. But there were so many changes. Having the Internet was the biggest change. The house was cleaner, for sure. It was like I could see Honey's new happiness reflected in the house. Even Macon and Lovie seemed different, more grown up. It was weird, because I felt like I hadn't changed at all.

And Dad . . . Mom said to me just before she left for deployment that she hoped Dad would find himself again on Dewees Island. The place where he grew up. But I think it was more than that. Though none of us said it aloud, we all worried he would never face the challenge of losing his leg. It made my stomach tighten thinking about it.

I blew out a plume of air. In the shadowy light, I took a final sweep of the room. At least here, in my room, everything seemed the same.

CHAPTER 3

The search for treasure is on!

I WOKE TO THE SOUNDS OF NOISY BIRDS CALL-ing to one another from the treetops outside the round window. I tried to fall back asleep, but the smell of bacon cooking downstairs lured me to the floor. Suddenly I remembered: Today was going to be epic. I quickly changed into my clothes and thought, *Operation Treasure Hunt is beginning!* I could hardly wait to see Lovie and Macon. I shimmied down the loft ladder, and the smell of bacon hit me again. My stomach grumbled loudly. Okay, all this could wait until *after* breakfast.

"Good morning, sleepyhead!" Honey said from her seat at the table.

Dad, sitting next to her, peeked out from behind a book. "Morning, Private," he said with a quick smile. He was still in his pajamas.

Dad and Honey were big readers. They always had a book nearby. Last summer, all Honey seemed to do was read. She didn't clean or cook much. This summer was different. She was always busy with her work at the Nature Center, her Turtle Team duties, keeping her house clean, and cooking for us.

It was hard to see Dad just sitting there. He used to be the one who got me up early with calls of *Rise and shine*. He was a runner, too, and even did triathlons. Since his injury, he just sat around—a lot. He said his prosthetic made him tire out quickly, or it was uncomfortable, but to me it felt like he just didn't care about anything as much anymore . . . including me.

"I hollered up to you to join us for breakfast, but you were out like a light," Honey said. She patted the place setting near her. "Come eat. I had to practically arm wrestle your daddy to keep his hands off the last slices of bacon."

I stuffed a crispy slice of it in my mouth, making sure to break off a little piece for Lucky, who was greeting me with a big wagging tail. After I finished, I slipped on my backpack and carried my dishes to the sink.

"I'm heading over to Macon's now. We've got a treasure hunt to plan."

"Don't forget your chores," reminded Honey.

"Yes, ma'am." I retrieved the garbage and recycling from the bin to carry down to the golf cart.

"Oh, Jake," Honey called after me. "You go ahead and use the lift to carry the trash down. But that's all, hear? I want you to get your exercise."

I beamed. "Thanks, Honey!"

I loaded the golf cart with the container for fresh water, the recycling, and the trash. I'd learned to be quick about getting my chores done so I could meet up with my friends. Last year I learned how to drive a golf cart, and this year I was driving *my own cart!* I backed out of the open space under the tall wood pilings of the house. It wasn't a garage. It was more a covered space on gravel. All the houses on the island were raised one story up on either cement blocks or wooden pilings in case of flooding. The tidal surge that came with big storms was a part of island living.

My first stop was the Trash and Recycling Center. It felt great to be back bumping along the dirt roads of the island. The roads were dry and dusty, and the sun shone hot above, but June was my favorite summer month because the days were not as sweaty as late July and August. On those days I'd come home from chores dripping wet from the heat and humidity.

As I drove, I kept my eyes open for critters, like deer, raccoons, and alligators. Especially Big Al. On the island, if an alligator decided to cross the road, all traffic stopped. One night a coyote crossed the road in the glare of my headlights.

A flash of white caught my eye, and I slowed for a closer look. A large bird landed on a pine limb about fifteen feet high, so close I could see the unlucky fish dangling from its big talons. The bird lifted its white head and stared at me, almost challenging, while its dark brown wings spread out and wiggled.

"Nice catch," I said to the osprey, and moved on.

I recycled the trash, picked up the mail and water, and returned to the Bird's Nest. After chugging water, I headed back out. I couldn't wait to see my friends. Dad was still in his pajamas, sitting in the recliner, reading.

"I'm going to meet up with Macon and Lovie," I called out.

Dad lifted his hand in a silent farewell, never looking up from his book.

I blew out a plume of air, then whistled for Lucky. To my surprise, Lucky didn't run to my side. He stood in the open space between me and my dad, uncertain. The dog turned his head to look at my dad, then whimpered.

"Go ahead," I said in a low voice. I knew his dog super hearing could hear me.

Lucky trotted to my dad and lay with a soft grunt at his feet. I watched my dad's hand slide down to stroke Lucky's back in what looked like an unconscious movement.

Macon's family house was twice as big as Honey's and was one of the nicest on the island. As I rode up the smooth, unrutted driveway, I noticed how all the shrubs and trees, though natural and wild, were trimmed so nothing smacked into the cart, unlike Honey's driveway. I wasn't jealous that the Simmonses were rich or had a fancier house. I was just amazed they could hire people to come all the way by ferry to Dewees to keep their road cleared and the wilderness pushed back. At home, I was the lawn care guy. I mowed the grass and cleared the driveway. I made a mental note to start clearing Honey's driveway this week.

Macon's house was gleaming white, with two large pillars on either side of the wide porch. Sweeping stairs led to the front door, where enormous blue pots were filled with colorful flowers. I always felt like I was stepping into a *Southern Living* magazine cover when I entered Macon's house.

I rang the doorbell, and two seconds later the door jerked open.

Macon's face looked flushed. "Finally! Come on in. Lovie's on her way." He shut the door behind me, kicking a pink toy out of our way. "Watch your step."

I stood gaping at Macon's house. Boy had it changed. Last summer it was like a hotel, all sparkly clean, white furniture, and flowers everywhere. Now it was baby central! Toys were everywhere—scattered over the floor, on the sofas, there was even one in a planter! Dirty dishes covered the kitchen counter, and a mound of unfolded laundry buried a sofa. A baby's high-pitched cry echoed through the house.

"Is she all right?"

Macon waved his hand with disgust. "Aw, she always sounds like that." He rolled his eyes. "Nap time."

"She doesn't sound very tired," I said.

Macon shook his head and bent over to pick up a colorful rubber block off the floor. "Help me pick up, would ya? Mama said I can't go anywhere till this place is tidy." He tossed the block into a small toy basket. "Mom's got a lot of work for me now."

I grabbed a few toys off the floor and tried to shoot them into the wicker basket. Macon laughed and did the same. The game was on! We raced each other to see who could make the most baskets with toys.

"Winner!" I yelled.

"Congratulations! You get to help me finish folding the towels." Macon smirked.

"Wow. Great prize," I replied sarcastically. "How does one little baby make so much mess?"

"Oh, *trust me*. You have no idea. Babies are a ton of work! And noise." He made a face.

I'd never heard Macon complain like that, and it surprised me, especially because last summer all he talked about was how excited he was to be having a baby sister.

Just as we finished, the doorbell rang. It was Lovie.

"Hey, guys. What're you doing?"

"Good timing," Macon muttered as he let Lovie in the house.

I went running to the door. "Wait. Let's get outta here before your mom gives you more chores."

"Good idea." Macon quickly wrote his mom a note and stuck it to the fridge. "Let's go!"

We laughed as our feet pounded down the stairs to our golf carts. Macon hopped in beside me.

"Where's Lucky?" Lovie asked.

"Oh, he stayed back with my dad. So," I said, putting my hands on the wheel, "where should we go?"

"Let's go to our spot on the beach," Macon said. "I haven't seen the ocean yet."

Lovie climbed in the back of my cart and leaned over the front seat. "You guys are in for a surprise." As we bumped along the dirt road, we passed just a few other golf carts. It felt like we were the only people here in the wild place.

We took turns telling stories about the past year, laughing, and poking fun at one another. Normal stuff. When I looked in their faces, I knew we all felt how good it was to be together again. Maybe I felt it more than anyone else. Moving to a new school, Mom out flying missions, and Dad being depressed, I missed my friends—more than I could tell them.

"Stop. Turn here!" Lovie yelled from the back seat of the cart. We had been so busy talking, I had almost zoomed right by the sign: ANCIENT DUNES BEACH ACCESS.

The sandy beach path was uneven and rutty from tree roots sticking up every which way. At last, we reached the boardwalk that crossed over a swampy area. Patches of tall wildflowers and tree stumps jutted out from the coffee-colored water. Finally, we reached the gazebo. This was our favorite gathering spot, after the Nature Center. It was also the site of our infamous Operation Coyote the summer before. I was sad to see that the gazebo's white paint was chipped and some of the screens were torn at the corners and flapping in the breeze.

"What happened?" I asked

"Storms. Wait till you see what's ahead," Lovie said, and then took off running down the walkway.

"And she's off . . . ," Macon said, then took off after her.

We followed, watching as she deftly leaped over a missing section of the boardwalk. We did the same, running by the small dunes blanketed with sea oats, yellow primrose, and other wildflowers. We burst out onto the beach. The whole sky seemed to open up over the ocean, and I couldn't help but feel my heart expand. Macon went running past me, so I hurried to catch up. The three of us stood shoulder-to-shoulder and let our gazes sweep the empty beach.

I was here on our beach, yet everything felt strangely out of place. Like, if this were a house, nature had rearranged the furniture. Some of the small dunes I remembered from last summer were just gone now. And the water's edge seemed closer than before. In fact, the whole beach seemed smaller.

"You've got the same look on your face I had when I saw it a few weeks ago," Lovie said. "You should see some of the other beach access paths. Osprey Walk is, like, totally gone."

"What happened?" I asked.

"It's sea level rise," Macon said as we began walking toward the shoreline.

I knew the human Google would have an answer. It was

one of the things that most impressed me about Macon. He knew something about a lot of things.

"I heard about that in school," I said.

"We're getting a lot of bad flooding now," Lovie said. "If a rainstorm hits Charleston, it's so bad people are riding canoes in the streets. Out here on the islands, our beaches are disappearing."

I looked out at the ocean. The waves rolled in and out softly, like a sleeping beast. It was hard to imagine the kind of power the ocean had when it was awakened and devoured the beaches.

Macon jerked his head in the direction of the beach path. "Uh, we've got company."

I turned to see a man wearing a tan camouflage bucket hat that drooped low over his forehead. He walked with a slow, unsteady gait from the beach path. He looked older than Honey and was slightly stooped. In his hand he carried a black metal contraption.

"Is that what I think it is?" I asked, watching him like a hawk.

"Dang," Macon said with awe. "That's a metal detector."

We watched as the old man reached the shoreline, then fiddled a bit with his contraption. At the bottom of the metal pole was a circular scanner. He held the pole with both hands so it stretched out in front of him as he began to walk. He seemed very intent, his head bent, as his gaze followed the contraption. Back and forth, left and right, he slowly, methodically, waved the metal detector just inches above the sand.

"He's got to be that guy!" I said to Lovie. When she looked

at me confused, I said, "You know, the man in the newspaper."

Her eyes widened and she took a few steps closer, squinting. Then she turned back to us and waved us closer. "Yes!" she said in an excited whisper. "That's him."

"The treasure hunter guy?" Macon asked, catching on.

When Lovie nodded, we all turned as one and watched the man.

"Binoculars," I said, tapping Macon's shoulder.

Macon slipped his from around his neck and handed them to me. I brought the binoculars to my eyes, focused, and brought Mr. Maynard into view.

He wore aviator sunglasses, the kind with mirrors that reflect the sunlight. Bony knees stuck out from under his khaki shorts, and below, white socks went clear up to his calf. Under his hat, wispy spikes of white hair fluttered like feathers. Focusing, I saw a web of red scars creeping up his neck on his left side and under his white, short sleeves.

"It looks like he's been hurt," I said in a hushed voice.

"Let me see," Macon asked, holding out his hand.

I gave him back his binoculars and Macon brought them to his eyes.

"Whoa . . ." He handed the binoculars, to Lovie. "Those are burns."

Lovie took her turn studying the old man, then slowly lowered her hands. "That's definitely Mr. Maynard. Harold Maynard. But the grown-ups call him Harry." Lovie kept her voice down as we all pretended to look at something in the water.

"He lives near my Aunt Sissy. He's kind of a mysterious guy. Keeps to himself mostly. One time, she told me—"

"Oh, watch," I interrupted her. "He stopped. I think he's found something."

Lovie handed me the binoculars, and I watched as Mr. Maynard hovered the detector above a section of beach. Then, setting it aside, he slowly kneeled down to investigate.

"He's digging," Macon said, his excitement ringing in his whispers.

"If he found the rest of the treasure already, I'll die," I said in a soft groan.

"Shhh," Lovie whispered. "What can you see, Jake?"

I peered through the binoculars again. "He's pulling something out of the sand."

Macon sucked in his breath, and I could feel Lovie clutch my upper arm. Then my breath came out in a short laugh.

"What?" asked Macon.

"It's a soda can," I said, lowering the binoculars.

Macon slapped a hand across his mouth, trying to smother the guffaw bursting out.

"Our treasure is still out there," I said confidently.

"For now," Lovie said with a tease. "Look at him. He's still searching. He's out here all the time. He never stops. Aunt Sissy said his house is filled with old treasures and historical stuff. All things that he's found washed ashore."

"Look, he's found something else," I said, peering through the binoculars.

Mr. Maynard stopped again and was going back down to dig. We moved closer to see what he was scraping at with the edge of his hand shovel. We all held our breaths when he put the shovel down to dig with his hands. He plucked something from the loosened sand, too small for us to see. After careful inspection, he tucked it into a shirt pocket. The shirt puffed and billowed in a gust of wind, like the strands of his hair.

"Did he just find another coin?" I whispered. My curiosity was at max level now.

"Let's go find out," Macon said, and took a step forward, but Lovie pulled him back.

"Don't. He doesn't like . . . well, anybody," Lovie said. "Aunt Sissy warned me to leave him be."

Old Mr. Maynard carefully, slowly, rose to stand. Then, suddenly, he swung his head to stare out in our direction, like he had that oh-oh feeling someone was watching him. And we were! His pale blue eyes were laser-focused on mine. I sucked in my breath, embarrassed I'd been caught staring. I quickly turned my head and pretended to see something in the small tidal pool nearby. Macon and Lovie did the same.

"He caught us staring," I said under my breath.

"Dang . . . ," muttered Macon, standing frozen beside me.

"Is he still staring at us?" I whispered.

Macon glanced over his shoulder. "Yup."

It was a stalemate. He just stood there watching us while we stood pretending not to notice him. Ants were crawling over my sandals, and I prayed they didn't bite. But I didn't move a muscle.

At last he must've gotten bored, because he moved on, swinging his metal detector left and right over and over as he walked along the shoreline.

"Let's go," I said, and took off, my heels digging in the sand as I raced across the beach. Macon and Lovie were right behind me. When we reached the golf cart, we leaned against it, panting.

"What's up with that guy?" asked Macon, catching his breath. "He's creeping me out."

"Do you think he's mad that we're watching him?" I asked, wiping sweat from my brow.

"Uh, yeah," Macon said. "He's treasure hunting. He doesn't want us spying on him. In case he strikes it rich."

I thought of his angry-looking scars and wondered how he'd gotten them. "You don't think he's . . . I dunno . . . dangerous? I mean, if we find the treasure," I asked nervously.

Macon didn't answer, but his eyes widened at the thought.

"I think he's . . . ," Lovie said slowly, "scary."

"Yeah. That dude is, like, Scary Harry," Macon replied.

I nodded in agreement and turned to take another look at the old man from our safe spot on the boardwalk. He was so far off in the distance now, I couldn't see much more than his slight figure.

"I wonder what he found out there."

"You think it's another coin?" asked Lovie.

"Could be." Macon snorted. "But it's probably just another soda can tab."

I felt fired up. I wasn't about to lose out on our treasure. "You guys want to find treasure this summer, right?"

"Of course," said Lovie. She looked surprised that I'd asked the question.

Macon made a face. "Duh!"

I grinned and climbed into the cart. "Then the search for treasure is on!"

CHAPTER 4

Finding your family history is kind of finding a treasure too

WE COULDN'T GET TO THE NATURE CEN-
ter fast enough. I raced the cart into the parking area and slammed on the brakes. I felt like
I had to practically stand on it as we skidded to a halt, spit-
ting gravel and scaring a few small birds out of a nearby
tree. We laughed as our feet pounded the wood steps up to
the Nature Center.

"Whoa, here comes the cavalry!" Honey exclaimed when
we burst into the room. "What's your hurry, kids?"

"Hi, Honey," I called out as I slipped my backpack off my
shoulders. "We're on a treasure hunt."

I made a beeline for the square wooden table in the corner. Honey had created this small meeting place under a window for everyone who visited, but with an eye for The Islanders. Honey knew this was our favorite place to work on our journals, identify animals and birds, and just hang out. Shelves of reference books framed the nook and gave it a private feeling. It was our very own headquarters.

Lovie perched on the edge of a chair, teetering forward with excitement. Macon tossed his backpack on the floor and grabbed a chair. It scraped the wood floor as he dragged it closer, eyes alert.

"I'm calling it," I said with a slap on the table. "*Operation Treasure Hunt* is on."

"Wait," Lovie exclaimed, and bent to pull her journal out from her backpack. Honey had distributed the same composition notebooks to them. Macon's was blue and Lovie's was green. Lovie opened her notebook and clicked her ballpoint pen. "Okay, ready."

"We need to be organized," I said. "Remember when we did Operation Coyote, we learned about coyotes and figured out what we needed to protect the sea turtle nest from them?" When they nodded, I continued. "I think we should learn about pirates."

"Yeah," said Macon, catching on. "Then we can figure out where that treasure might be. Or else we'll be digging up the whole island."

Lovie giggled as she wrote down *Things We Need.* "Okay, so the first thing we need is a book about pirates."

"Not just pirates," I said. "Pirates that came to South Carolina."

"Yeah, but the gold doubloon was found *here.* On Dewees Island," said Macon.

"Wait!" Lovie leaped from her chair and hurried to a different section of the room.

"Man," Macon said with a shake of his head, "she only has one speed. Fast."

I laughed because it was true. Lovie was a firecracker of energy and island knowledge. It's what made her so much fun to be around. Of all of us, she was the most attuned to nature. I figured that was because she grew up on Isle of Palms and drove the small motorboat from there to Dewees Island every day in the summer to spend the day with her Aunt Sissy while her mom worked. Both Macon and I were city kids transplanted here in the summer. Macon was from Atlanta. I had come from McGuire Air Force Base in New Jersey.

Lovie raced back to our corner with a book in hand. "Okay, guys, listen up. There's some great stuff here." She rustled the pages and settled in to read.

Blackbeard was one of the most infamous pirates. His real name was Edward Teach

41

and he was from England. Blackbeard was over six feet tall. His nickname came from his beard, which started at eyebrow level and went down to his belt. The beard was supposedly tied into braids.

"Cool," Macon said, eyes gleaming.

Honey walked closer, another book in her hand. "You know, it's said he put lit fuses in his wild black beard to make smoke waft around him and look fierce."

"Whoa!" we all exclaimed.

"He sounds as cunning as Captain Jack Sparrow," said Lovie.

"You know Captain Sparrow was not a real pirate, right?" Macon said.

Lovie lifted her chin. "Of course. But he did have braids and all. . . ."

I wanted to roll my eyes. Those two were always arguing. "Does it say anywhere in that book where his treasure *might* be?" I interrupted.

While Lovie flipped through her book, Honey opened hers.

"As a matter of fact," Honey said, "here's something you might find interesting." She cleared her throat and read.

In early June of the year 1718, Blackbeard arrived at the entrance to Charleston Harbor with four ships and over four hundred pirates.

"Whoa!" exclaimed Macon. "That's, like, an army of pirates."

Honey nodded, and I could see she was pleased at Macon's reaction. "Imagine this," she said, then continued to read.

> Blackbeard sealed off Charleston Harbor. Not only that, but every ship that tried to enter or leave the harbor was captured. It was one of the largest pirate attacks to have ever occurred on the American coastline.

Honey closed her book, eyes gleaming. "Follow me, children."

We scrambled from our seats to where a large mural filled a wall. It showed a larger-than-life Dewees Island and, smaller, the surrounding area, including Isle of Palms, Sullivan's Island, and Charleston Harbor. Honey and her friends had worked long and hard creating the map mural of the island. Nearby, a collage of photos was on display showing different animals that had been spotted on nature cameras.

"How many cameras are out there?" said Macon.

"Not many. We only have them in areas where we need to keep an eye on the wildlife. The four-legged *and* the two-legged kind," Honey said with a wink.

On the map mural, Honey had placed small pins that marked where all the sea turtle nests were located, where coyotes and other animals were spotted, and even where Big Al was last seen hanging out.

I was proud of Honey. My grandmother had really stepped

up as the librarian of the Nature Center. She'd transformed what was a dimly lit, cluttered room into this cool hub. Now it was bright and cheery—a lot like Honey. I thought that sometimes, change could be a good thing.

We clustered around Honey as she pointed to the mural.

"Let's start with what we know," Honey began. "Blackbeard left Charleston with loads of loot and traveled to North Carolina. So, let's follow his path." She began dragging her finger on the mural along Charleston Harbor and into the ocean along the barrier islands. She lowered her arm.

"Blackbeard had a lot of valuable items that had to be split with his crew. He was a selfish pirate and ruthless. He wanted to hide his treasure before he had to share it with the other pirates, or before anyone stole it from him. So . . ." Honey crossed her arms and asked us, "If you were a pirate looking for a spot to bury some of your treasure—and you were in a hurry—where would you go?" She lifted a finger. "Remember! You're traveling north." We clustered closer to the mural, all of us considering what we would do if we were the pirate captain.

"Sullivan's Island?" Lovie asked.

"Yes, Sullivan's Island comes first," Honey replied. "There are some who say the treasure is buried there. And maybe it is." She turned to face us. "But consider this. Back in the early 1700s, when Blackbeard was sailing, Sullivan's Island was notorious for pest houses."

"Pest houses? Like a place for cockroaches and mice?" I got the shivers just imagining them.

Honey leaned against her desk. "No. For diseases. There was nothing the early colonists feared more than disease. More than war or even hurricanes. The slave ships were coming into Charleston Harbor, one after the other. So the city built small houses on Sullivan's Island to hold the enslaved people in quarantine before they were transferred to Charleston to be sold." She paused and said solemnly, "Some two hundred thousand enslaved people were quarantined on Sullivan's Island."

I sat back in my chair, stunned by that number. I had learned about slavery and the Civil War in school. But thinking about how all that history happened just ten miles away made it come alive. Real. I felt my stomach twist.

Macon sat silently, his brows furrowed. "My mama's family has lived in South Carolina for a long, long time. She said the new museum is helping her discover her ancestors."

"Tessa mentioned that to me. And your mama's not alone. Genealogy is a big part of the museum. As many as eighty percent of African Americans can trace one ancestor through the Port of Charleston. That's why it's important that the new International African American Museum is being built right here. A lot of family mysteries will be uncovered."

"Finding your family history is a kind of finding a treasure too," Lovie said. "It's important to know about your family. The good and the bad."

I looked at her and knew she was thinking about her father in prison. I made a mental note to ask her if she ever got a letter from him.

"Speaking of treasure . . ." Honey tapped the map mural on the wall with her fingernail to bring our attention back. "We still have to figure out where ol' Blackbeard might have stashed his treasure."

Intrigued, I stepped closer to the mural and studied it, chin in my palm. Macon and Lovie joined me. We stood shoulder-to-shoulder, looking up.

I spoke first. "I'm guessing if Blackbeard knew there were all those pest houses with slaves and guards on Sullivan's Island, he would skip it."

"And probably the Isle of Palms too," added Lovie, "because they're so close. And because ships sometimes docked there. He wouldn't want anyone watching."

"I know!" Macon yelled out. He went to the mural and ran his finger farther north. "If he skipped those two islands," he began, "the next closest island would be—"

"Dewees!" the three of us said, in unison.

"Bingo." Lovie turned to face us, eyebrows high. "So maybe the treasure is indeed on Dewees."

"Good thinking," Honey said. She walked to a bookshelf and picked up sheets of paper. "Here are maps of the island," she said, passing out a printed copy to each of us. It was the same map that everyone got when they visited the island.

"Thanks, Honey," I said, and we raced back to our table. "We needed a map."

"Okay, let's get organized," Macon said, getting excited.

Lovie pulled out her notebook and read aloud as she began

46

to write under the heading *Things We Need.* "Number one, books on pirates. Check. Number two, a map of the island. Check." She tapped her pencil on the table. "What else?"

Macon leaned forward. "I know exactly what we need." His dark brown eyes sparked with an idea. "A metal detector!"

CHAPTER 5

Teams take turns

THE BUZZ OF CICADAS FILLED THE STAG-
nant air at the main dock. It was the sound of summer
in the South.

"Are you sure the package is arriving today?" Lovie asked as
she mindlessly tossed a few stray periwinkle shells from a
wooden platform into the water below.

"Yes," Macon replied with a groan. He'd answered her
question at least two times already. "My mom showed me the
notification, and it said it was coming this morning." He wiped
the sweat off his face with his shirtsleeve.

I squinted into the direction of the ferry. Lucky lay beside my feet, panting. The humidity was as thick as a swamp today. The midday sun was at its highest point in the sky, and even in the shade, sweat rolled down my neck. The package hadn't come on the earlier ferry, and we'd been waiting for nearly an hour.

"That package better be on the next boat. I'm melting out here."

Lovie jumped to her feet, pointing. "I see it!"

The white double-decker Dewees Island Ferry was right on time. It docked as it did every hour, loading and unloading families, guests, construction workers, groceries, and delivered packages.

Lucky trotted down the dock and wagged his tail in excitement as the mate jumped from the ferry to tie up. We waited at the end of the dock as all the passengers disembarked. At last, the first mate handed Macon a brown box with his name on it. Macon was so excited, he gave the box a quick hug and held it overhead like he'd just won a trophy.

"Meet you at the Nature Center!" I called as we sprinted to our golf carts. Lucky hopped up in his usual spot beside me and we drove straight there. We gathered at our table behind the bookcase, a.k.a. The Islanders Headquarters. Macon started tearing open the box, then stared inside with dismay. "Everything's in pieces."

"Ugh, this looks complicated," I said, staring down at what looked like a hundred tiny parts to be assembled.

Lovie searched the box and found the printed directions.

She spread them out on the table. "Come on, we can do this. We just have to follow the steps."

"I know where Honey keeps her toolbox," I said. I went to fetch it from the utility closet and hurried back. I pulled out a screwdriver. "It's not so bad. We can do this."

Macon scratched his head, then sat at the table and read through the directions. "At least there are drawings," he said, studying them. "They make sense."

"Where do we start?" asked Lovie, leaning in.

Step by step, we followed the directions. I was pretty good at putting the sections together, but we all smiled and felt the thrill of success. I could tell Macon and Lovie were getting into it.

"How'd you learn so much about building stuff?" Macon asked.

I shrugged. "My dad," I replied. "He's the handyman of the house and he likes building things. He taught me a lot."

"My dad is good at doing chores around the house," said Lovie. "He calls it his Honey-Do list."

Macon laughed and shook his head. "My dad calls up the handyman."

I thought back on all the times my dad included me in his projects and taught me the names of the different tools and how to use them. That was all before the accident. He didn't do many chores anymore, and I realized with a pang that it was one more part of my dad that I missed.

I looked at Lovie, who was studying the directions. "Have

you heard from your"—I paused to remember what name to use—"your biological dad? Did he answer your letter?"

Her hands stilled on the papers. After a brief pause, she shook her head. "I don't want to talk about that right now." She looked up, and her eyes appealed for understanding. "Okay?"

I focused on the screw I was tightening. "Oh yeah, sure." My cheeks felt hot, and Macon didn't say a word. I didn't mean to put her on the spot. It occurred to me that I wasn't the only one dealing with a father problem. I'd have to remember to ask her about it later, when she was ready to talk.

"I think that's it," I said, straightening.

"Good job, Islanders," said Lovie.

Macon picked up the metal detector and inspected it. "Looks good," he proclaimed. "Let's test this baby out."

"Operation Treasure Hunt begins," I shouted with a fist bump to Macon, then to Lovie.

The sun was a fireball high in the sky, and the heat seemed to roll off it in waves. Just beyond, the ocean appeared cool and inviting. It was low tide and the beach spread far out. Ahead of me, Macon wasn't budging from his metal detector. I felt sweat roll down my spine and looked longingly at the ocean. I wanted to run and dive into the waves. But this mission was more important.

Lovie and I were following Macon as he walked along the high tide line of the beach, where the incoming waves might have left treasures. He was strong enough to hold the metal detector in one arm as he walked, leaning forward slightly, methodically waving the long-handled detector back and forth a few inches above the sand.

"Where's the breeze today?" Lovie fanned herself with her hand. "It's so gross out."

Macon stopped moving, waving the metal detector in smaller swipes. Lovie and I froze, ready to take action.

"False alarm," he yelled out, not taking his eyes off the ground.

"He's like Lucky when he's sniffing the ground," I said with a short laugh. "Nothing distracts him."

Lovie giggled beside me. "Yeah, he just can't stop. I mean never ever . . ."

"Yeah." His determination was one of the things I liked most about Macon. But this morning, he was hogging the tool. Maybe it was the heat, but we were beginning to feel annoyed.

I could see sweat marks seeping through the back of Macon's light green T-shirt, which seemed almost too small for him. It made his broad shoulders look even bigger, showing the ridges of muscles, too. He was taller and bigger this summer. *No fair*, I thought, as I looked down at myself. Still just a skinny kid, wishing for a growth spurt.

"Watch this, Jake." Lovie tapped my arm. "And keep count," she said over her shoulder as she took off jogging several steps and then cartwheeled across the damp sand in her shorts and yellow one-piece swimsuit. She was like a bright starfish rolling down the beach with tanned, outstretched arms and legs. I couldn't help but smile at her. When she sprang to a stop and turned toward me, I noticed that her hair was in a ponytail, not the usual long braid. She swung her hair off her shoulder and smiled real big back at me.

"How many did I do?" she shouted.

"Uh . . . sorry! I lost count," I shouted back, which was kind of a lie because I had forgotten to count. I was too distracted by a thought: *Lovie is not only the coolest girl I've ever known, but also the prettiest.*

"Thanks for nothing," she teased. "Hey, y'all. Want to go in the ocean? It's so hot today."

Before I could respond, Macon yelled out to us. "You guys! Come quick. I got a hit!" He used the tip of his flip-flop to make a small circle in the hard, wet sand, marking the spot. "The meter is going nuts right there!"

Lovie and I caught up to him and dropped to our knees. We began clawing at the spot with our fingers. It hurt.

"This won't work. Be right back!" Lovie scrambled to her feet and dashed to the high tide line. After a moment's search, she ran back and handed me a shell. "Use this. Nature's perfect digging tool."

I recognized the cockle shell from the Turtle Patrol. The team used this kind of shell when they dug to open up sea turtle nests. It sure was easier.

"I found something!"

Macon and Lovie stopped and watched.

I proudly held up the first treasure we pulled from the sand. Lovie giggled.

"Great," Macon said with a roll of his eyes.

I looked at what I was holding, and my shoulders slumped. A soda can tab. "We're no better than Scary Harry." I tossed it over my shoulder.

"No littering." Lovie picked it up and stuffed it in the pocket of her jean shorts.

"Hey, it's good sign," Macon said. "It means the metal detector is working."

"That's right," Lovie said encouragingly. "And it was just our first hit. Treasure awaits, me hearties."

"Aye, aye!" I replied.

"This pirate wants a turn," Lovie said, reaching out for the metal detector.

Macon quickly pulled it back from her grab.

"Come on, Macon," she pleaded, but her tone was sharp. "You've been using it for at least fifteen minutes."

"I will. In a minute," Macon said, and put the headphones back on. "I'm just getting used to it."

Lovie dropped her hand with a huff of frustration. We didn't speak as we followed behind Macon, and I felt a new tension. She was right. Macon wasn't sharing the metal detector, but the truth was, it belonged to him. It seemed fair that he had a chance to try it out first.

Macon worked the detector for another fifteen minutes. He found a couple of lost pennies, a rusty nail, and half of a pair of scissors. He wiped his brow and at last seemed done with the detector.

"Not much treasure," he said with disappointment.

"*Now* can I try?" Lovie asked in a testy voice.

Macon's face clouded, and I could tell he still didn't want to let go of the detector. "Fine . . . but don't mess with any of the buttons on the indicator screen, got it?"

"Yeah, yeah," Lovie said, walking up with her hand out. "We've only been watching you for, like, half an hour now."

Macon begrudgingly handed Lovie the metal detector. She did a little ball step of excitement, then got all serious, wiped her palms, and took hold of the detector.

"You're holding it all wrong," he cried, grabbing the detector from her. "Like this." He showed her how to position her hand.

With her brow knitted, Lovie held the metal pole as Macon had shown. She started walking along the sand, waving the instrument like a metronome.

Macon slapped his hand on his forehead. "You're doing it all wrong. Stop walking so fast. You've got to go slow."

Lovie puffed out her breath in frustration. "Okay."

I could hear she was getting angry. "Hey, she's doing okay," I told Macon.

But he wasn't listening. A few minutes later Macon shouted, "You're too fast. Go slow!"

Lovie stopped abruptly and swung her head around to look back at Macon. "Give me a break! All you're doing is complaining."

"Am not. You just aren't listening. Anyway, your turn's up. Let Jake try it."

"I just got it!"

"You've had it for almost ten minutes."

"Fine." Lovie tightened her lips and thrust the detector in my direction.

It hadn't been ten minutes, and I wanted to stop the fighting, so I said, "It's okay. Lovie, you keep using it."

"I don't want to," she snapped, and handed me the machine. Then she turned on her heel and walked away without a word.

"Lovie!" I called after her. "Come back. Seriously, it's still your turn."

"Let her go. She'll be fine," Macon said.

"Teams take turns," I fired back.

"Hey, I gave her a turn. And now it's yours." Satisfied with his explanation, he immediately started giving me directions about how to hold the metal detector.

I tried to follow Macon's directions, but I was distracted by Lovie leaving in a huff. I glanced over my shoulder to see her sitting on a log, looking out toward the ocean. Her arms were crossed. With her being mad, using the metal detector wasn't as fun anymore. I began sweeping it slowly, left to right, but Macon was hovering, watching the lights and needle move on the control box.

"Dude! You're breathing on me," I said.

Macon stepped back, just slightly.

Now I was getting frustrated too. "I've got this, okay?" Suddenly a beeping noise turned my attention to the sand.

"I found something!" I turned to Lovie, waving my arm at her. "I found something!"

Lovie jumped up to come help, but Macon was already on his knees, digging with the big shell. She crossed her arms again and just watched.

"Whatever it is, it's bigger," he said, excitedly. A moment later he pulled up the treasure. "Another soda can." He scrunched up his face as he held up our latest find. I laughed and was glad to hear Macon join in. Lovie was watching us, only she wasn't laughing. She wasn't even smiling. I held up the can and shrugged.

"I'm going home," she called out, and turned to walk away.

"Wait. I'll drive you back." I handed the metal detector to Macon.

"It's okay. I'll walk," she called, and headed toward the beach path.

I watched the heavy-heeled way she walked and wondered if she was mad at me, or Macon, or both of us. "Maybe we should go try to talk to her?"

Macon didn't reply. He was laser-focused on the metal detector, swinging it back and forth across the sand. Scratching my head, I looked back toward Lovie, but she was already gone.

I don't know how long we stayed on the beach, but it was long enough to uncover a couple of rusty fishing hooks, another penny, and a broken pair of sunglasses. The coolest find was a green Matchbox toy car. I was sitting on the sand, sorting out the stuff. Macon sat on his haunches beside me.

"We should start a collection," I said. "We might find—"

Macon interrupted. "You know these dudes?" He jutted his chin in the direction of the beach path.

I looked up from our pile of stuff and saw two boys headed our way. They looked to be about our age, maybe a bit older. They wore brand-name clothing and walked with a swagger that reminded me of the popular guys from my school who were always showing off, trying to act super cool.

"No." I hardly knew anyone on the island, and there were definitely very few kids. As they drew closer, I saw that one boy was as tall as Macon, but skinny. His blond hair was thick and fell over his eyes, like he had just styled it. He had to be from a city, I thought. My hand went to my own head. I felt the short stubble of my *high and tight* haircut that my dad and I got every summer. The other kid was his exact opposite— short but hefty. *Built sturdy like a wall,* my dad would say. His black hair defied gravity, jutting straight up and out.

"Hey," I called out with a slight wave of the hand, trying to be friendly.

They stopped a few feet away, and though I couldn't see their eyes behind their sunglasses, I felt the icy sweep of their gazes.

"Whatcha doing, dork detectives?" the tall one said, and laughed. It was that insulting kind of snort that had me clenching my jaw as I felt my spine stiffen.

"We're not detectives," Macon said in quick defense. "We're trea—" I elbowed Macon so he wouldn't say too much. "We're doing a beach sweep."

I was impressed at his fast thinking.

"You mean trash collector training," the tall one said, as he slapped his friend's back with a laugh.

The short one lowered his sunglasses to eyeball our findings. "Boring," he pronounced before they walked off.

Between laughs and slaps as they kept walking, I heard the word "nerds" and felt my cheeks flame. "Jerks," I muttered at their backs.

Macon said, "Don't worry about those pea-brains. We've got a bigger problem coming our way." A quick jerk of his head drew my attention to another person. The camouflage boonie hat was all I needed to see. I sucked in a breath. "Oh no, it's Scary Harry," I whispered.

"He's coming right for us," Macon muttered through gritted teeth. "We're dead."

I measured the old man's slow, tottering steps toward us through the sand with my breaths.

"Hey, you kids," the old man yelled out as he approached. In one hand he carried his metal detector. In the other hand, a small nylon bag. When he drew close, I could see his hand wrapped around the pole. Two of his fingertips were missing, and his hand was covered in scars. My stomach flipped, and I wanted to run.

"What are you doing with that thing?" He shot a glance at our metal detector.

"Uh, it's a gift from my mom, sir." Macon looked down to fiddle with the knobs.

"A gift, you say?"

"Yes, sir."

Scary Harry snorted, eyeing the both of us and then our items laid out on the sand. I shifted my stance, feeling uncertain about what was happening.

Macon cleared his throat and gave me a quick look of confusion.

The old man's lips curled into a lopsided grin as he speared us with a suspicious gaze. "You're hunting for treasure, aren't you?"

We shifted our eyes to our feet. "We're just . . . uh . . . playing around," I said. "Uh, Macon, we better go. It's late."

"Yeah," Macon said, and turned off the metal detector.

"Bye," we yelled simultaneously, and sprinted back to the gazebo. Neither of us dared look back.

CHAPTER 6

Don't judge a book by its cover

EVENINGS AT THE BIRD'S NEST WERE quickly becoming my favorite time of day. Me, my dad, and Honey were comfortable just being together. Outside our windows the cicadas and crickets sang, the chorus rising and falling loudly like an insect concert.

Tonight, Chief Rand joined us for dinner. Honey had fried up chicken and made her special coleslaw and mashed potatoes. Rand and Dad sat on the sofa, laughing and talking, just old friends having a good time catching up. When Rand laughed, the sound came from his belly and shook the house. I looked at Honey and saw her gazing at my dad, her eyes all soft and a small smile playing at her lips. I could tell she was happy her boy was back home for a visit. And that he was laughing again.

"You boys want some dessert?" Honey called out. "I made your old favorite, Rice Krispies treats."

Rand leaned back in the cushion and patted his belly. "You're killing me, Mrs. Potter!" he said with a laugh.

Honey chuckled as she carried over a platter of treats. "I couldn't resist. It was your favorite when you were boys."

"Well, *I'm* still a boy," I said, and dove in to grasp two bars as she passed me. "I love them too."

Honey set the tray on the coffee table, then went to her leather chair and sank into the cushions with a sigh, propping up her feet on the ottoman. She picked up the book that was on the table beside her. I headed for the desk in the corner with my backpack. I pulled out the map that Honey had given me and hunched over it to study.

"What's got you so interested over there?" Dad called out.

I turned around in my chair, letting my arm rest on its back. "It's just a map of the island. But, Dad, it's cool because we're using it to help us search for treasure!"

Chief Rand craned his head from the sofa to look at me. "What? Don't tell me you're hunting for Blackbeard's treasure?"

I felt a little deflated and said defensively, "We sure are. Mr. Maynard found a gold doubloon. Didn't you hear?"

"The whole island's been talking about nothing else. Of course I heard," Chief Rand said, and his tone was encouraging. "I've had a devil of a time keeping people from trying to come on the island to search for treasure. Doubloon or no, Dewees is still a private island."

"Yeah," I said. "You keep them away. That treasure is mine!"

"Spoken like a true pirate," Honey said, lowering her book to her lap.

"Don't tell me Ol' Man Maynard is still around," said my dad. "He was ancient when we were kids."

Honey bristled and waved her hand. "He's only a bit older than I am, so careful of your words. And it's not polite to call him that. He's a fine man."

Dad gave her a skewed look. "Come on, Mom. He's a little weird."

I heard Rand chuckle, but he didn't say anything.

"I think he's scary," I said. "We call him Scary Harry."

Dad and Rand burst out laughing. I joined them, until Honey shot me a sharp look.

"Don't you go on with that disrespectful talk. Harold served in Vietnam. He's a war hero. He rescued three soldiers." She lifted her hand to show three fingers. "Saved their lives and got some terrible burns in the process. Not to mention other injuries, too. So what that he keeps to himself? Seems to me he's earned his privacy."

Dad's face was still, but his eyes were alive with emotion. "I didn't know that."

"It was all in the newspaper. After he found that doubloon," Honey explained, then turned to me. "Don't judge a book by its cover. Harold Maynard's scars should serve as a reminder of his sacrifices. And our family knows a thing or two about that." She looked firmly at my dad and then at me.

"Yes, ma'am," I replied.

Dad nodded as well. Only the muscle of his clenched jaw moved. Rand sat there wide-eyed, looking at all of us.

In an upbeat tone, Honey said, "The children have taken a great interest in pirates. They've read books on the Charleston siege and charted where they think Blackbeard may have buried some treasure. I did some more reading myself," she added. "Most folks believe his treasure is in North Carolina, where he scuttled his ship *Queen Anne's Revenge*. But I think the kids are right to imagine other possibilities. Like maybe he dumped at least some of it before he got there. To keep it for himself."

"You know they discovered the *Queen Anne's Revenge* a while back." Chief Rand paused to think. "It was 1996. That ship revealed a lot of secrets and artifacts."

"And the treasure?" I asked.

He shook his head. "No treasure. That, kiddo, remains a mystery."

I smiled with relief.

Rand turned to my dad. "Remember when you and I hunted for Blackbeard's treasure back in the day?"

My dad rubbed his jaw. "That was a long time ago, but yeah," he said, nodding with a smile of memory. "I remember now. We really were into it. In fact," he said, "we even had a map."

"A treasure map? You had Blackbeard's map?" I jumped from my chair.

Dad laughed and shook his head. "No, no, not Blackbeard's map." He laughed again. "If we'd had that we'd be rich now. That treasure is thought to be worth millions."

"Wow!" I already began to think how I'd spend my share.

"Red and I, we had a map of our making."

Chief Rand threw his head back in laughter. "No one calls me that name anymore, 'cept you!"

Dad grinned. "Well, that nickname lives on for as long as that hair of yours stays red."

"What map?" I repeated.

"Not just any map," Chief Rand said, leaning toward me with his elbows resting on his knees. "That map was the product of several years of hunting. We found some coins, if I recall."

"Really?"

"Oh yes."

"Doubloons?"

"I don't think they were doubloons. They weren't gold. But I do know they were old, and we hid them and made a map to find them again."

My interest peaked. "So do you think you know where it is?"

"The treasure or the map?" my dad asked.

I shrugged. "Both, I guess."

My dad scratched behind his ear. "I have no idea where Blackbeard's treasure is. But the map to *our* treasure . . ." My dad looked at me. "The map wasn't up in my room?"

"Nope." I knew because I went through everything in my dad's room the summer before. When my dad was injured and no one knew how bad, I wanted to feel close to him, so I read most of the books on his shelf, studied his journal, and even started my own journal. "Believe me, I would've remembered a treasure map."

Dad looked at Chief Rand, puzzled. "Do you know what happened to the map?"

Rand scratched the red beard that grew along his jawline. "Now, that there's a good question. For sure I don't have it. But I think I know where it might be."

"Where?" I blurted out with excitement.

"We each had a box of our favorite things. Our own treasures, so to speak. I have mine. I kept it for sentiment's sake. I don't have the map, so we must've kept it in your box, Eric. After all, you drew it."

My dad's eyes gleamed. "That old metal box. I remember it now. It was all bent and rusted at the hinges, but I loved it. I kept my treasures in it." He looked up with a wistful smile. "Yes, I remember now. I kept the treasure map in it. But if the metal box is not in the loft, I don't know where it is."

"Do you think it's still in the tree fort?" asked Rand.

Dad's gaze clouded. "The tree fort?"

"Come on, Eric," cajoled Rand. "Don't tell me you don't remember our tree fort? We practically lived in it that one summer."

A grin crossed my dad's face. "Oh yeah. Wasn't that the year I broke my arm? It's all coming back to me. Our tree fort.

I bet that's where it is. Safe from plunderers"—he turned to Honey—"and snooping mothers."

She laughed and opened her book back up. "I'm going to ignore that accusation."

"Let's go get it!" I exclaimed.

Rand and my dad looked at each other.

"Do you remember where the tree fort is?" my dad asked. "'Cause I don't."

Rand scratched his beard again, then shook his head. "I sort of remember the general area it was in. But gosh, I haven't thought about that thing in a long time."

"But you live here," Dad joked.

"That was over twenty years ago! Do you have a clue how much an island can change in that time?"

"But we can find it," I said. "Right?"

"We can try," said Dad.

CHAPTER 7

Operation Island Invaders

THE NEXT MORNING, I COULD HARDLY FIND a place to park when I pulled up to the Nature Center. Usually there were no more than two other golf carts, but today there were five.

Inside, the center was busier than I had ever seen it. People buzzed about looking at the displays and posters. Honey was talking to someone about the number of turtle nests so far this season. "Five," I heard her say, as she glanced my way, giving a wink. I waved and weaved around people to get to Lovie, who was sitting at our table.

"Hey! What's up with the crowd?" I plopped down in the chair next to her.

Lovie just shrugged.

"You okay?" I asked as I pulled my notebook from my backpack.

She rolled her eyes. "I'm still mad at you."

I shot her a look of surprise. "What did I do?"

"Y'all totally left me out of the treasure hunt at the beach. I thought we're a team. The Islanders, remember? Instead, you and Macon made me feel like the odd one out."

I wanted to defend myself by saying I did try to include her. To remind her that she's the one who stomped off. But I didn't get to say any of it.

"Ahoy, mateys!" Macon yelled out with his face contorted, using a really bad pirate voice. "Me headquarters be overrun with varmints. Arrrrrrgh!"

I busted out laughing. And I saw Lovie crack a smile too.

"Ye be the worst pirate imitation ever!" I stood up, pointing my pencil at Macon like a sword. "Go walk the plank, scally-wag. I'm yer cap'n now!"

A few people looked over at us. Their eyebrows showed total confusion at our performance. At a stern glance from Honey, we slunk low into our seats around the table.

"It's too crowded to talk in here," Macon said as he scanned the room. "You know, this stuff is private."

"Yeah," I agreed. "We don't want anyone to find out what we're doing. How about we go to the gazebo?"

"Let's go."

Macon and I were on our feet when I noticed Lovie hadn't moved. "You coming?"

"I don't know."

"Why not?" Macon asked.

Lovie looked down at her hands. Her voice was low. "Because you haven't apologized yet."

"*Apologize?*" Macon asked in a voice so loud Honey turned her head again and scowled. "For what?" he said, lowering his voice.

"For being so rude to me yesterday."

Macon's face went blank, and he looked at me. I shrugged, not wanting to get in the middle of another argument between them. "Rude?" Macon asked, his eyes wide. "What're you talking about?"

Lovie tightened her face in frustration. "Do you know what you are, Macon Simmons? A metal detector hog. That's what. You wouldn't give me or Jake a chance to use it. You hoarded it all for yourself."

"First of all, you're wrong. I did share." He turned to me for validation. "Didn't I?"

I met his gaze, shrugged, then said in a low voice, "Once. For five minutes, before you grabbed it back."

Macon looked chastened. "Really? Oh." He paused. "I didn't know." He turned to Lovie. "Sorry. But . . ." He paused, then blurted, "It's, like, brand-new. I . . . I guess I was a little excited to use it."

"A little?" Lovie said with a snort.

"I said I was sorry. Okay?"

Lovie's fingers twiddled her turtle necklace as she considered his apology. Then Macon blurted out, "But you ran off, remember?"

"I didn't run off. I simply went home."

I didn't think Macon sounded very sincere, and I didn't think Lovie was cutting him any slack. So I stepped in. "Come on. Let's go."

Just as they rose from their chairs, Honey cornered us.

"Children! Hold on a minute. I want you to meet some visitors who I think you'll enjoy getting to know."

She took one side step, revealing the two boys Macon and I met on the beach the previous day. Their eyes were gleaming, like they thought all this was a big joke. Every muscle in my body tensed. I felt Macon discreetly kick my foot.

Lovie ran her hand down her long braid, laying it on her shoulder.

"Meet Eddie Teach and Andy Wang," Honey said. "They're cousins, and their families are renting a house on the island this month." She turned to Lovie. "They're staying at the Harris house, which is just a stone's throw from your Aunt Sissy's house."

Lovie looked up at the boys and smiled brightly, which was weird because she was mad and frowning less than a minute ago. The two boys shifted their attention right to her.

No! Don't be nice to them, I wanted to shout at her. Those boys were bad news.

"Hi," Eddie said, with a quick wave.

"Nice to meet you," Andy said, with an excess of politeness.

I was shocked they were acting like they had never met us before.

"Hello," Macon and I mumbled back. Lovie just kept grinning.

"I was wondering," Honey said. "Would you kids give the boys a proper tour of the island? They're visiting from Washington, D.C., and this is their first visit to Dewees."

Macon and I glanced at each other and took an uneasy step back. I rammed my hands in the pockets of my shorts, "Uh, we can't. Not today. We have, uh, plans."

Honey's face registered surprise, and maybe some disappointment. "Oh."

Lovie broke the awkward silence. "I'd be happy to show them around."

Stunned, I swung my head to look at her. Her eyes were on the two boys as she fiddled with her sea turtle necklace.

"I'm Lovie Legare." She smiled a quick, almost shy smile. "And these are my friends, Jake and Macon."

Honey clapped her hands together with satisfaction. "Well, I think this is just lovely." She handed the boys each a map of the island and a blank notebook. "I'm leading a nature journaling class once a week. The schedule is by the door. I hope you'll join us. The other children participate."

"Thank you, ma'am," the blond boy, whose name was Eddie, said. He cast a quick glance my way, and his eyes were brimming with held-back laughter.

I wanted to crawl inside a bookcase and hide. Honey kept calling us "children" like we were five years old.

Honey kept on going. "There's directions inside those composition books. Keep them handy and bring them to the session. I'll help you learn all kinds of things about our wonderful little island." She pointed over to the activity board. "Speaking of which, you'll find all kinds of activities listed. Feel free to join in on any of them. You're more than welcome."

"Yes, ma'am. Thank you so much," Eddie said with a wide grin.

Honey returned the smile, pleased, then walked back to her work pinning information on the mural.

Eddie moved in closer to Lovie, his blue eyes shining on her. "So, where do you want to go?"

I watched her face blush.

"I don't know," she said, and then giggled.

"If you don't know, we sure don't."

This time when the boys laughed there wasn't any mocking. But I cringed inside. The turtle tank glowed behind the boys. They didn't see Pierre clawing at the glass for attention. I guess Lovie didn't notice either.

"Do you have a golf cart?" Lovie asked them.

"Yeah. Sure," the shorter, dark-haired boy answered, whose name I'd remembered was Andy.

"Okay, I know where I want to show you first."

In typical fashion, Lovie took off walking fast toward the door. The boys hurried after her. As they neared the door, I watched Eddie set his notebook down on the nearest table before exiting. He met Andy's gaze and made a thumbs-down gesture.

As Andy neared the table, he dropped his notebook on top of the other one. Catching my gaze, he said in a low voice, "See ya, dorks."

"Can you believe them?" Macon said. "What fakers! Acting all nice in front of your grandmother. I don't trust them. And what's with Lovie?"

I could only shrug because I didn't know. She was sure acting weird.

As soon as the door clicked shut, we hurried over to it and peered out the window. Lovie was walking toward the row of golf carts with Eddie and Andy on either side of her. I could see her hands move in the air as she talked, the way she did when she was excited. The boys looked like they were hanging on to her every word. I felt my stomach tighten and a new simmering that felt more like worry than anger.

As I watched their golf cart speed off down the road, an idea struck. Eyes still on them, I asked Macon, "Remember when you were following me in the woods last summer?"

"Yeah."

"I think it's time to use those tracking skills for a two-man covert mission." I glanced at my friend.

Macon's eyes sparked with understanding. "Yeah," he replied, this time with more gusto. "Operation Island Invaders is about to commence."

CHAPTER 8

Don't tease the gators

"**W**HERE ARE THOSE BINOCULARS?**"
Macon was tearing through his closet, shoving and pushing things out of the way. A box toppled from a closet shelf, making a big crash. "Grr! They were right here!" He tapped his palm on his forehead. "Think. Think. Think."

I stood in the center of his room holding everything else he had dug out for our secret mission: walkie-talkies, jumbo stick of chalk, can of bug spray, water bottles, and snacks from his kitchen pantry.

"How do you find *anything* in here?" I asked. His room looked like a shipwreck.

Macon paced his room, somehow managing to nimbly move around his messy piles of clothes. "Ah ha!" He tossed a lone dirty sock off his windowsill. Underneath lay his binoculars.

"Can we go now? My arms are getting tired!"

We passed by Macon's mom and baby sister on our way through the living room on a beeline for the front door.

"Where are you two headed?" Mrs. Simmons called out. Her head was wrapped in a purple turban that matched the long, flowy dress she was wearing. She was sitting on the sofa beside Faith, who played on the floor. Toys were scattered everywhere.

"Treasure hunting," Macon replied. "Gotta go."

Suddenly the phone rang. Mrs. Simmons answered it, then snapped her fingers in the air to get our attention. We looked at each other and groaned.

Mrs. Simmons placed her hand over the phone. "Macon, I've got to take this call. Please, just for a minute." She started walking to another room for privacy. "Watch your sister while I'm on the phone." And just as she was about to close her office door, she added, "Oh, and please change her diaper."

"Number one or number two?" he called out.

His mom shrugged and shut the door behind her.

Macon moaned and plopped down on the couch in front of his sister, Faith. She was leaning her belly against the coffee table, looking up at Macon adoringly.

"Diaper duty is the worst."

"It can't be *that* bad."

His baby sister looked up at me and giggled and went back to slapping at musical buttons on a toy.

Macon smirked and asked, "What do you know about diapers? You're an *only* child." He slowly shook his head. "Those were the days."

"Hey, you were so excited to have a baby sister."

"Yeah. What did I know?" He pulled back his shoulders like a man on a mission and pointed to a basket filled with diapers across the table. "Grab one of those. And that white box of wipes."

I fetched the baby's diaper basket like Macon asked. He pulled a bandana from the box of toys nearby and tied it around his face, covering his mouth and nose.

"*What* are you doing?" I laughed.

"Brace yourself."

I started to laugh again when a stench punched me in my nose as he opened up the diaper.

I slapped my hand over my nose and mouth. "What. Is. That?" I gagged at the sight.

Macon yelled back, "Quick! Get the wipes."

I frantically yanked out one wipe after another, holding my breath as I handed them to him.

Macon leaned far back and turned his head, making a gagging sound, which made me gag.

"Quick! Drop this in that white trash can." He passed me the balled-up dirty diaper like it was a hot potato.

"Ew! It's warm!" I screamed as I ran it to the trash can. I felt like I was disposing of a live grenade.

I watched Macon slip a fresh diaper under his sister's bottom and close the Velcro tapes with the speed and ease of a pro. He was pretty good at it, and I realized that being a big brother was *really* hard work.

When he was done, he picked Faith up from the sofa. She wrapped her chubby arms around his neck and hugged him close. Macon's frown lifted to a smile, and he spoke softly to his sister as he gently returned her to the floor. He bent to pick up a toy and wiggled it in front of Faith to make her laugh.

Watching, I thought Macon didn't really mind being a big brother so much. And that maybe being a brother could also be pretty cool.

Later, loaded with gear, we took off to track down Lovie and the Island Invaders. We checked all six beach access paths on the island. No luck. We tiptoed up the steps of the Nature Center like ninjas and peered into the windows. Nobody was there. Not even Honey.

"Maybe she took them kayaking," I suggested.

Macon shook his head and added X marks to our map on the spots labeled Nature Center and Crab Dock. "I counted the canoes and kayaks when we zoomed by the crabbing dock."

"Impressive observation skills." From our vantage point on the high deck of the Nature Center, I squinted over at the main dock. Lovie's boat bobbed gently in the water. "They didn't go out on her boat."

"Cross that off too." Macon wiped sweat off his face with the end of his T-shirt and then scanned the area with his binoculars. "I cannot believe we haven't found them yet. It's so hot!"

A drop of sweat rolled down off the tip of my nose onto the map, leaving a splat mark on the area labeled POOL.

"I know where they are!" I exclaimed.

Electric golf carts make it easy to creep up on someone because they hardly make a sound on the dirt paths, as long as you avoid sticks and potholes. I parked my cart a distance away in the shade so we wouldn't be seen. Macon and I bent low and scrambled toward Huyler House, the community center. We hurried past the tennis and basketball courts to the ground level under the main house, where we liked to hang out. The screened-in area was cool in the shade and kept out pesky mosquitoes. We looked around and were disappointed not to see anyone sitting at the picnic tables or hammocks or playing at the pool or Ping-Pong tables.

"I wonder where they are," I said.

Squeals and laughter made us freeze in a crouched position.

"That's Lovie," I said.

"We need eyes on them," Macon whispered.

I nodded and pointed my index finger up above my head. Without another word spoken, we crept toward a staircase.

On the second-floor deck, we had a good view of the pool and deck. The palmetto trees and wide wood columns gave us good cover. Macon pulled out his binoculars.

"Roger that. I see Lovie and the Invaders."

I didn't need binoculars to see the three of them huddled together by the shallow end of the pool. Andy was holding a long metal pole with a net.

"What's going on?" I asked, careful to keep my voice low. "They look pretty excited about something. Something's in the pool."

"Yeah. I'm trying to get it in focus." Macon slowly moved the dial of his binoculars pressed to his eyes.

I watched Andy slowly raise the net out of the pool water. Something in the net wiggled and thrashed.

Andy and Eddie were hooting about their find.

"What are you doing?" I heard Lovie scream. She threw her arms up by her head. "You shouldn't do that!"

"What is it?" I pressed.

Macon lowered his binoculars.

"Gator," he slowly mouthed.

"Nah, it's too small."

"It's a baby gator," Macon confirmed, and thrust the binoculars at me.

Pressing the binoculars to my eyes, I quickly confirmed Macon's claim. A baby alligator, no more than two feet in length, was trapped inside the pool net.

"Look at me! I'm Jungle Jim," Andy said. "I just rescued a

lost gator." He lifted the net higher in the air. "Bring it here. I want to hold it," Eddie said, grabbing the rim of the net to pull it closer.

"You're not serious, right?" Andy asked. "It's a gator."

"Chill out. It's a baby." Eddie thrust his hand into the net and slowly lifted the small, wriggling gator out, holding it behind its head. "I held one of these during a family trip down in Florida, remember?"

Andy's mouth fell open. "Yeah, but those baby gators had their mouths taped shut."

"Oh." Eddie paused for a moment, then shrugged off that fact.

"Come on, guys," Lovie said. "Put the alligator back in the net. We should go get Honey. She'll know what to do with it."

"It's almost two feet long," Andy said, pulling out his cell phone. "It *is* kind of cute." He lifted his phone to take a picture. "Smile!"

Eddie brought the gator closer and smiled for the camera. The baby gator wiggled, trying to free itself from Eddie's grip.

"Stop it," Lovie shouted at them. "You can't handle it like that. You'll hurt it. Besides, it may be small, but it's got sharp teeth. A lot of them."

Eddie stretched out his arm to hold the gator farther from his chest. "Open up the net." Andy stepped closer, and Eddie placed the alligator in the net. It lay motionless.

"What do we do now?" Andy asked Eddie.

"I don't know. Maybe keep it as a pet? At least while we're here this month."

"Yeah. It *is* cute."

"You *can't* keep it," Lovie said matter-of-factly. "It's against the law."

"Who's going to know?" Eddie asked. His tone was challenging.

Macon and I shook our heads, watching in nervous suspense from our lookout spot. "What in the world is a gator doing in the pool?" I asked.

"Maybe it got lost," Macon said. "Wandered from a pond."

I took a turn looking through the binoculars. "I hope that gator bites them."

Lovie bent over the net, inspecting the alligator. "We have to get it back to its mother, poor thing," she said. "Or it will die. There's a pond right behind Huyler House. I'll bet that's where this little guy came from. We can carry it back and let it loose. I just hope its mother will find it."

"But I want to keep it," Eddie said.

"You can't keep it," Lovie argued back. "It will die."

"Fine. We'll put it back." Eddie took the pool net handle from Andy. "Let's go. This guy doesn't look so good anyway."

Macon and I ducked behind one of the big columns on the porch above as they turned and headed back toward the community center. Thank goodness we'd come upstairs. I held my breath, hoping they wouldn't notice us on the deck above them.

When they headed out toward the pond, Macon and I hoisted our backpacks and crept down the stairs and scurried after them in stealth mode. When we caught up to them at the pond, they were already at the edge of the water and were standing in knee-high grass.

We stayed back, hiding behind a thick cluster of prickly shrubs. Insects hovered over the water, and occasionally a fish jumped up to feast. In a nearby tree, a few egrets clustered in the branches. Smack in the middle of the pond was a wooden raft. And on that raft, as still as a statue, was an enormous alligator.

"Hey, look!" Eddie said, his voice lowered to a whisper of awe. "That's the biggest alligator I've ever seen."

"It's like Godzilla!" exclaimed Andy.

"It's Big Al," Lovie informed them. "Only the biggest alligator on the island. He's the king bull around here. Nobody messes with Big Al."

"Let's get out of here," Andy said, taking a step back.

"We're okay, if we're careful," Lovie said. "Alligators are cold-blooded animals, so they like to lie in the sun to warm up. It helps with digestion, too. So if we leave him alone, he won't come after us. But we don't want to disturb him because alligators are super fast. You can't outrun him if he's after you."

"Don't worry," Andy said. "I don't want Godzilla coming after me."

"It's the gator you don't see that you have to worry about," Lovie said.

"Let's dump the gator and get out of here." Andy slapped at his arm. "The mosquitoes are eating me alive."

The baby gator started making high-pitched chirping cries from deep in its throat.

From our hiding place, Macon and I looked at each other with knowing eyes. "Uh-oh," I said.

"Hey!" Eddie laughed. "The gator sounds like a laser gun."

"I think it's, like, crying," Andy said. "Poor little guy."

Lovie started scanning the pond. "Put it down, quick!" Lovie urged. "It's calling for its mother." When Eddie didn't move, Lovie shouted, "Hurry! That mama will come fast. And . . ." She gasped. "Oh no. Big Al is looking right at us."

From his perch on the raft, Big Al's head moved ever so slightly toward the sound. Macon and I tensed. That was a lot of movement for Big Al.

That got the boys moving. Eddie opened the net, and Lovie reached in and picked up the gator with both hands. It was chirping like mad now. She stood at the bank, searching, then hurried to where a streak of mud revealed where an alligator had slid into the water. She carefully set the baby gator on the mud, then took several big steps backward. The little reptile scurried away fast, making a splash when it hit the dark water.

"Let's get outta here!" Lovie started running to the golf cart. "You don't want to meet its mom . . . or Big Al."

The boys ran at her heels and jumped on the golf cart. We watched as they zoomed off. Looking back at the pond, I spotted a long, dark streak head toward the bank. I didn't speak, but nudged Macon and pointed. He turned, and I heard his breath suck in when he spotted it, then the pair of eyes above the waterline. Mama alligator had heard the cries and was coming for her baby.

"Let's get out of here!" I hissed.

Macon and I slowly backed away, turned, then hightailed it back to our golf cart.

"I want to rat out those Island Invaders so bad," he said, climbing onto the cart.

"Yeah, me too, but think about it, bro. On one hand, it'd be great payback. But what if Andy and Eddie got the same kind of punishment that we did last year?"

"Dawn Patrol . . ." Understanding washed over his face.

The summer before, we got in trouble and our community service was having to walk the beach with the Dewees Island Turtle Team at dawn *every day* searching for turtle nests. What we thought was going to be torture turned out to be pretty cool. We spent a lot of time together on the beach and even found my dog, Lucky. Dawn Patrol was *our* thing.

"It's too risky," I said. "Besides, what could we say that they did wrong? They rescued a baby alligator from the pool and returned it to the marsh."

"They'd be heroes!" Macon shook his head in the palm of his hand.

"Right." I sighed, feeling defeated. "Score one for the Invaders."

"For now." Macon snorted. "How dumb are they, messing with gators? If they keep teasing the alligators, Big Al will settle the score. Did you know that the saltwater crocodile has the strongest bite of any animal?"

I smiled to myself, thinking Mr. Google was back with his fun facts. "No, really?"

"Yep. Crocodiles and alligators haven't changed much since the days of dinosaurs. They're all instinct and stealth hunters." He wiggled his brows. "Like us."

We laughed as he glanced back at the pond, checking for the gators.

"It's quiet, but we should go," Macon said. "They'll leave us alone if we leave them alone."

"Roger that." I switched on the golf cart. *Don't tease the gators* was the top rule of the island. Especially not Big Al.

Before I drove off, I took a final look back over my shoulder. I saw Big Al still sitting on the wooden float in the center of the pond, like a king on his throne.

Big Al !!

CHAPTER 9

Landscape changes over time, season by season, like we do

THE NEXT MORNING, A LOUD THUD WOKE me up. That and the sun pouring in from my large, round window. Yawning, I looked down and saw my dad's old leather journal lying on the floor. I must've fallen asleep reading it. As I stretched, words from his journal popped into my mind: *tree fort, metal box, key, map.*

The summer before I had discovered his nature journal, written when he was eleven, like I was then. I'd learned so much about the way my dad explored Dewees Island, how he drew the animals, plants, and birds he saw, then identified them. He also wrote about what happened to him each day.

Dad was really good at putting his emotions into words.

This year I was reading his other journals, written when he was older. I'd waited to read these because I wanted to be the same age my dad was when he wrote them. And now I hoped Dad left clues as to the whereabouts of his tree fort.

And I think I scored.

I dressed quickly in my excitement, bending to swoop the journal off the floor as I headed downstairs. Lucky was waiting for me at the bottom of the loft ladder, his tail wagging so hard his bottom moved with it.

"Morning, Lucky. I'm happy to see you too," I said as he licked me. I gave him a good scratch in return. "Want to go on a treasure hunt with me?" He barked. "Good. It's going to be epic. But first," I said as I headed to the kitchen, "breakfast."

"Good morning, early bird," Dad said, looking up from a book at the kitchen table.

He was still dressed in pajama bottoms and a faded Army T-shirt. Seeing him like this, I felt my excitement wither in my chest. Dad was an *up and at 'em* kind of guy. Both he and Mom rose with the sun to exercise, then showered and dressed for the day. *Spic and span.* Those were expressions my mom liked to say.

When I arrived at the Bird's Nest last summer, the house was gloomy, even dirty, with books everywhere and dirty dishes in the sink. Honey rose late in the morning and didn't dress until even later, preferring to pad around the house with a book in one hand, coffee in the other. The whole house felt her sadness. To be honest, I was pretty mopey too, missing my mom and dad. But over the summer we both helped each other find the courage to change. Honey was back to her old self, large and in charge. She was already up and out with the Turtle Team. Hot coffee simmered in the pot, and biscuits and butter and dewberry jam were laid out for me and my dad. Those small gestures were like love notes she'd written for us.

To see my dad still in his pajamas, I wondered what I could do to cheer him up.

I filled up Lucky's dog bowl with food and joined Dad at the table. I was encouraged to see the book wasn't a book after all, but the new composition notebook Honey had given to him.

"Hey, Dad," I said, sliding into a seat beside him. "I found some clues in one of your old journals upstairs. You wrote all about your old tree fort and the treasure you found, and the map. And a key. And . . ." The words raced out of my mouth as I buttered a biscuit.

"Slow down, son." Dad closed the journal and pushed it aside. He rubbed the brown stubble on his chin and leaned back in his dining chair. "What's this about my old journal?"

I pulled his old journal from my backpack. I opened it to where I'd stuck a pencil in it as a bookmark and slid it toward him. "It's all right there. You wrote you found some treasure. But," I said with emphasis, "you didn't say what it was. Was it the coins you told me about?" I shoved half of the biscuit in my mouth and chewed quickly, hungry and eager to know more.

Dad thumbed through the journal as I continued talking through mouthfuls of biscuit. "And where is it?"

The space between Dad's eyebrows scrunched up. His *thinking face,* Mom called it.

"Jake, remember, that was decades ago! I haven't a clue where that tree is."

The front door opened, and Honey shuffled in, kicking off her sand-crusted sandals into the basket. She was dressed in a Dewees Island Turtle Patrol Team uniform. Lucky ran over to greet her.

"Found a nest this morning!" she called out. Her face was pink from the heat and climbing the stairs, but she was beaming.

I grinned from ear to ear. "Good morning, Honey."

"When you're out there hunting for treasure, we could use some help checking the nests," Honey told me.

I popped the last bite of biscuit in my mouth. "Okay, sure. We'll do it."

Honey went to the kitchen and poured herself a glass of water. She drank thirstily, then walked to our table. "What are you two up to?"

"Nothing much," Dad said in a flat tone.

At the same time, I blurted out, "We are trying to locate the tree fort!"

The difference in both of our voices was apparent to Honey. She looked at me, then looked at Dad, her eyes hooded with concern. "You're not dressed yet, Eric?"

"What's the hurry?" Dad replied. "I don't have anywhere to go."

I saw Honey's eyes flash, but she took a breath, then said, "Seems to me your son has somewhere he'd like you to go."

Dad turned and looked out the window.

"I remember that tree fort project of yours," Honey said in an upbeat tone. "From sunup to sundown, you and Rand stayed out in the woods, working on that fort."

I looked at Dad, but he didn't reply. He just picked up his mug and took a sip of coffee.

Honey walked back to the kitchen and grabbed a coffee mug from the cabinet. She poured steaming coffee into her mug and kept up her cheery tone. "You boys absolutely refused to show me the fort. You know, if you hadn't been so secretive, I might've remembered where the tree was myself." She chuckled, stirring in sugar and milk, took a long sip, then added, "If my old brain remembers correctly, I think you wrote down the location in some secret message. So no one would ever find it. It was a riddle or something, right?"

"Well, how would you know, Mom?" He looked up, and a crooked smile eased across his face. "Sounds like someone was reading my journal."

"I'll never tell." Honey pretended to lock her mouth shut with her fingers.

I sighed in relief that the tension was over and Dad was smiling again.

"Do you at least remember where the tree *might* be?"

"Sorry, son. When you're young, you think you'll never forget such things. But you do."

"Amen to that," Honey added.

Dad shook his head. "Truth is, it's kind of hard for me to accept that I can't remember where the fort was. It was so important to both me and Red."

"Don't be too hard on yourself," Honey said. "Landscape changes over time, season by season, like we do. What with storms, and climate, not to mention new houses being built, any one of those could have felled that tree."

"Oh." My disappointment rang in my voice.

Dad reached over to slip an arm around my shoulder; then he looked at me, eye to eye. "How about this? I promise I'll read through my old journals. Cover to cover. From what you say, there'll be something in there that will jog my memory." His hand patted my shoulder. "We'll find that tree fort."

"Well, isn't this a fine start?" Honey said.

Before she turned her head, I thought I caught a flash of tears in her eyes.

The day turned out to be sunny, without a cloud in the blue sky. I swept away the dirt and sand from my golf cart, then whistled for Lucky. As I unplugged the cart from its charging station, Lucky jumped up to his usual spot beside me.

The July Fourth holiday was approaching, and island residents were arriving with family and guests in tow. I passed more carts than usual along the bumpy road as I made my way to Macon's house. Macon came rushing from the house when I pulled up. The plan was to meet up with Lovie so we could keep working on our treasure hunt.

"Charged up and ready to go!" Macon patted his metal detector gear like it was a prized possession. "I remembered to bring a hand shovel, too." He looked over his shoulder toward the house. "And I mean go! Before my mom calls me to change another diaper."

"Roger that. Hold on to Lucky," I said, and backed away for a fast getaway. As we bounced along the main dirt road, I noticed a familiar golf cart parked by the crabbing dock. I pulled over to the side. "Look, I think Lovie's here."

"What's she doing there?" asked Macon, craning his neck to see the dock behind all the shrubs.

"Stay here, boy." I patted Lucky's head and quickly looped his leash around one of the cart poles. "I'll be right back." He whined, and I kissed the top of his furry head.

We walked onto the short dock that jutted out over the marsh. Lovie was at the far end, lying on her belly. Her braid and arms dangled down over the edge. I was stunned to see Eddie and Andy were also there, doing the same thing.

Macon shot me a look with his brows raised.

"Hey, Lovie," I called as we approached. "What are you doing?"

"Hold on," she said, never looking up at me. She held a long-handled net in her hands.

Macon and I leaned over to check the water out.

"Got him!" Lovie yelled, quickly getting to her knees. She

lifted up the net. The other boys jumped to their feet to peer into the net.

"Nice catch, Lovie," Macon said. "That's a big one."

"Thanks." Lovie smiled at the compliment.

"It's gross looking," Andy said.

"No, it isn't. It's a crab," Eddie said. Then he grinned. "They taste great." He cast me a look that said, *Who invited you?*

I narrowed my eyes in reply.

"Actually, it's a stone crab. The largest kind on the island," said Lovie. "And yes, they are delicious, but you don't eat the whole crab. Only one claw. Though I get all soft thinking about pulling one claw off a stone crab."

Eddie pulled out a short reed from the bank and, bending, poked at the barnacles on the crab's shell. Immediately, the crab stuck out both of its thick, black-tipped claws in self-defense.

"Be nice," Lovie warned. "You don't want that claw to clamp down on one of your fingers."

"I'm not worried about some stupid crab," Eddie replied.

I caught Lovie rolling her eyes as she bent to gently toss the crab back into the water. I was glad to see that I wasn't the only one annoyed with these Island Invaders. But I wondered why she was spending the morning with them, especially after what they did at the pool yesterday.

Splash! Splash! Splash!

I turned to see Andy on his belly whacking at the water's surface with his fishing net.

"What in the world are you doing?" Lovie asked.

"Trying to catch the little blue crabs down here." His face was twisted with frustration.

Lovie and I laughed, knowing that Andy wasn't going to catch a thing making all that noise.

"You're pretty much scaring *every* crab away with all that thrashing," I said. "And FYI, splashing can also attract alligators. Just saying."

Before Andy could reply, Macon called out with excitement. "Hey, guys! Come check this out!" He hurried farther down the dock and pointed out across the water.

We gathered by his side and followed his pointed finger to see a small furry, brown head glide through the water. It swam in an undulating motion.

"It's not that Godzilla gator again, is it?" Andy asked, stepping back from the dock's edge. "Can that thing jump onto a dock?"

Andy's question actually made me wonder, *Can alligators jump? Or climb a tree?* I'd have to look that up and add it to my nature journal. I looked over at Macon, the walking Google.

Suddenly the animal slipped under the water, disappearing. "Where'd it go?" Lovie asked.

We all scanned the water, looking for signs of moving ripples or air bubbles that would tell us where the critter was.

Eddie broke the tense silence when he called out, "See that white bird over there in the weeds? Who wants to bet I can hit it with this?" He pulled a slingshot from his back pocket with a sly smile.

"No way. Don't shoot at it," I warned.

"You'll get us all in a lot of trouble. Dewees Island is a bird sanctuary," Macon said, emphasizing the word "sanctuary." "Do you even know what that means?" he added.

"Yeah, yeah, yeah. Of course, I know what sanctuary means."

Macon squared his broad shoulders. "Then you know it means 'protected.' As in animals are not shot at with slingshots."

Eddie merely snorted with a shake of his head.

Macon's eyes narrowed. "If you're so smart, you'd know those aren't weeds," he said, making air quotes with his fingers. "That's Spartina grass."

Eddie rolled his eyes at us. "Okay, nature nerds, I don't need a science lesson." He pulled a broken oyster shell out of his pocket and placed it in his slingshot.

"You better not dare shoot at that bird," called out Lovie. Her face was growing red, and it wasn't from the heat. "It's a great white egret. And it's *his* home."

"I won't try to hit the bird." He took aim. "I just want to see it fly."

"Wait! Stop!" Macon yelled. "Look! That animal's back. Right there near the egret."

The little brown swimmer had popped its head up again. This time, it had a small silver fish hanging from its mouth. We watched the startled egret stretch out its long wings to take flight, its long black legs dangling. Then the mystery creature let its body rise to the surface of the water to float on its back, holding the fish in its little pawed claws.

"Oh. My. Gosh!" Lovie exclaimed, pulling out her phone and pushing the record button. "Y'all, it's a wild river otter! I can't believe I'm actually seeing this. Isn't he cute?"

"Yeah," I said, smiling and looking at Lovie. Her hands were on her cheeks in wonder. I remembered last summer when Lovie told me about river otters living on Dewees Island. But she had never seen one. Except for the otters that lived at the South Carolina Aquarium, where her mom worked.

Suddenly, I saw Eddie's shell fragment launch across the water like a bullet. *Plunk!* It splashed into the water just a few feet shy of the otter. As fast as lightning, the otter disappeared under the water, leaving the fish floating.

Lovie shrieked in fury. "Why did you do that?"

"You could kill something with that thing," I yelled angrily, taking a step toward him. "What is your problem?"

Eddie walked closer to me, narrowing his eyes. Suddenly I was looking *up* at this guy who stood a whole head taller than me. I realized this kid could pulverize me in front of everyone right now.

"What's *your* problem?" he challenged back, sticking his nose close to my face.

Action conquers fear. My dad said that a lot in the months after his injury. I stood my ground and stared back at him, squeezing my hands into fists so tightly my fingernails dug into my palms.

Eddie stared me down for what felt like an entire minute. Then he backed off and released a short laugh.

"Nah! I'm just messing with you!" he said, slapping at my shoulder as he took a step back. He dug a small piece of gravel out of his pocket. "Just having a little fun." He squinted an eye to line up his shot. "I'm not going to hurt anything."

He pulled back the rubber strap with the pebble in it. Before he could release it though, Macon stepped up to Eddie. They matched each other in height, but Macon dominated him in overall size. Macon put his hand smack in front of the slingshot, still pulled taut.

"Cut it out. *Now.*" Macon growled out the last word.

Eddie raised his chin. "Who's going to make me?"

Macon looked at him and curled his lip. "Really?"

The rest of us held our breath, unsure what would happen next.

"Children!" An adult's voice rang out.

Eddie quickly tucked his slingshot into his back pocket.

"Are y'all blind?"

I turned to see Honey stepping off her golf cart. She was coming right for us.

Eddie ran his other hand through his hair, smiling. "Hi Mrs. Potter."

I rolled my eyes. *What a total suck-up,* I thought.

"Hello, Eddie." Honey's gaze swept over us. "Get your tails off this dock. Don't you see there's a gator moving in? Go on, now. Off the dock right this minute!"

Andy scurried like a marsh rat while the rest of us followed Honey off the dock onto the road. Then, as one, we looked across the water to spot the gator. It looked like a dark, lumpy log floating in the creek.

"Do you see those white poles jutting out of the water?" Honey pointed out straight ahead of us.

"Oh, yes, ma'am, I do," Eddie said, faking interest.

"If gators are on this side of those poles, you must leave the dock immediately. It's the rule, and it's there for your safety." She turned toward me. "Jake, you should know better."

Her words stung. If it wasn't for these jerk Island Invaders, I *would* have noticed the gator. Through gritted teeth, I said, "We were just getting ready to leave."

"Just as well," said Honey. "Jake, your father's looking for you. And, Macon, your mama asked me to tell you to check in. And you boys"—she turned to face Eddie and Andy—"I could use your help at the Nature Center. I need two strong boys to help me with moving bookcases." She smiled in that way that made it impossible for the boys to weasel out of it. "There'll be cookies afterward."

"Okay . . . ," they mumbled.

"Come along with me! I'll give you a lift." As she turned on her heel to head for her golf cart, the boys' fake expressions dropped and they shuffled their feet to leave with Honey.

Macon and I slid a glance at each other and had a hard time not laughing out loud. We didn't need to say anything. Eddie's and Andy's faces said it all.

Lucky barked with excitement when we returned to the cart. Macon and I climbed into my golf cart with Lucky sandwiched in the middle. Lovie hopped into her golf cart. I watched her take one last, longing look at the water in search of the otter before she pulled away.

Honey's cart pulled up beside mine. "I recommend you hurry back to the house. Your daddy said he's got some news about the tree fort."

Macon and I looked at each other with wide eyes. I took off faster than you could say "gator!"

CHAPTER 10

Storm's a'coming

MACON AND I LAUGHED ALL THE WAY
back to the Bird's Nest. Honey had no idea how
many points she'd scored with us by recruiting
those Invader boys to help her. *Sweet redemption,* Macon had
called it. Lovie drove ahead of us, because, well . . . fast and first
is the way she rolls.

When we pulled up to the house, a red pickup truck was
parked in front. On the driver-side door in silver lettering, it
said DEWEES ISLAND FIRE DEPARTMENT.

"Why is Chief Rand here?" Macon asked.

"No clue," I said, and shrugged.

We ran up the front steps of the house together. Bounding through the door, we followed the sound of deep voices and hearty laughs to the back porch. Dad and Chief Rand were talking together, each with a bottle of soda in hand. I grinned at the sight. Seeing my dad look so . . . happy was a nice surprise.

Chief Rand stood up to greet us first. "Well, look what the cat dragged in, Eric. Our favorite islanders!"

Dad raised his hand. "Hey, son! I didn't realize you were bringing the troops." He welcomed everyone. "Go grab yourselves a soda, too, and come join us."

Lucky went bananas with excitement at having all of us together. I thought his backside would fall off from all the tail wagging.

After we got settled on the porch, I noticed my friends' gazes shift from my dad's face down to his legs. He was wearing cargo shorts, exposing all the parts of his prosthesis. They didn't stare, but they weren't too cool about it, either. I could tell they weren't comfortable. A metal rod started just below where his left knee would be and went down into his sneaker where his foot would be, if he still had one. He usually wore pants because he didn't like the stares and awkward glances from strangers. I held my breath, hoping their stares didn't ruin my dad's mood.

"You wanted to know about the old tree fort and treasure, right?" Dad asked, tapping on his old journal. It was laid open on the wooden table.

"Yes!" I said, with a mix of relief and excitement.

We leaned forward, eager to learn every detail.

"Here's what we've got." Dad laid out a map of the island that identified everything on it—the roads in gray, house lots in yellow, and wild empty lots in light blue. Next to the map, one of his childhood leather journals lay open on the table.

Rand stretched over the table to draw a quarter-sized circle on a green space of the map just off our road, Old House Lane.

"We figured it's got to be somewhere on this side of the island." He pointed. "We think in this area. It was all a long time ago, but Eric and I remembered we were looking for a place away from houses and golf cart traffic." He straightened and crossed his arms. "Pretty much, it's a good guess."

Dad lifted the journal and looked at us. "But we have this. I have to admit we were stumped. But when I was reading the journal, I found this riddle. I wrote it to help us remember the fort's exact location."

Rand chuckled. "To protect its location from invaders."

"Yeah, we can relate," Macon said.

I nodded. "Yeah."

"Y'all know what a riddle is, right?" my dad asked.

Lovie shot her hand high above her head. "Ooh, I know!"

"This isn't school," I said in a drawl.

"You can blurt out the answer." Macon laughed.

She stuck out her tongue. Then, laughing at herself, she

said, "I'm just excited." She turned to my dad. "A riddle is a question or statement that is like a game to figure out the answer. It has clues."

Rand said, "That's right. Here's an example. What is black and white and read all over?"

We looked at each other, but no one knew the answer.

"A bleeding skunk?" asked Macon.

"Gross," Lovie said.

Rand laughed and shook his head. "A newspaper. Get it?"

"Oh," we all said at the same time, and pretended to laugh.

"Red, read . . . see what I did there?" When we just stared back, Rand shook his head. "Tough crowd."

"So, once we figure out the riddle, we'll find our map to the treasure, right?" I said with confidence.

"That's the plan. The riddle is pretty good, if I do say so myself," Dad replied. "Now listen up. I will read it through, but I warn you, it's long." He laughed self-consciously. "I was eleven. . . ." He pulled the journal closer and cleared his throat.

To find me you need to know
X marks the spot is the way to go.

Not on the ground. Near the sky!
Find the tall ones who bend way up high.

Turn straight to the northern tide.

Then walk west because the tree must hide.

It's disguised as a huge beast
With big ogre feet and arms that stretch east.

Around her waist is a rope.
Use it to climb with strength and with hope.

Don't fear you're not strong enough.
Use the steps to climb all the way up.

Go where a wise owl might be.
There you'll find the treasure from the sea.

Dad lowered the journal. He seemed pleased with himself.

"*You* wrote that, Dad?" I asked, impressed.

"It's really cool, Mr. Potter," Macon said. "And you're right. That's one long riddle."

Lovie cocked her head and scrunched up her face. "Yeah, but it doesn't make sense. Where is it?"

"That's the point of the riddle," Dad explained. "We have to figure it out."

"Uh, you mean, you don't know?" Macon asked, eyes wide. "But you wrote it."

Dad looked at Rand and they both laughed. "Yes, sir, I did. I'm hoping it will all come back to us when we get out there."

"Out where?" I asked.

Dad rose from the table, gathering the papers and the journal in a swoop. "Follow me!"

Armed with our island map, freshly marked to show the likely site of the tree fort, we set out on a golf cart parade. My dad led the way with Chief Rand riding sidekick and Lucky in the rear. The Islanders hopped in my golf cart. Our emotions are high. We were off on the treasure hunt at last!

"This is so great!" Lovie said, leaning in from the back seat, giving my shoulder a squeeze. "I mean, I can't believe they are looking for a treasure map they made when they were kids. That was way back in the 1990s."

"Dad and Chief Rand said they found some old coins and made a map to mark where they found them." I looked to my right before turning left onto another path, still following Dad and Chief Rand. "My dad said he stuffed that map in an old treasure box and hid it in the tree fort."

Macon was holding his metal detector tightly in the seat next to me, the headphones draped around his neck. "Maybe this little beauty will come in handy." He turned back to Lovie. "And I promise to let you use the metal detector this time, okay?"

"You better," she said, poking his shoulder, smiling wide.

"I'm sorry I hogged the fun last time," Macon offered.

I looked at Lovie in the cart's long rearview mirror and

watched a smile spread across her face before she leaned in from the back seat and gave Macon a hug. *Apology accepted*, I thought to myself.

"Brake!" Macon yelled, gripping the side of the golf cart. I slammed on the pedal and swerved to the left to avoid crashing into the back of Dad's cart. We skidded to a stop right next to his cart. I closed my eyes in relief and released my breath. Then I looked over at Dad, giving him a weak smile. "Bad brakes," I called out, feeling sheepish.

"Nice evasive action!" Chief Rand said, jumping out of my dad's cart. "Need a hand, Eric?" he asked, walking over to the driver side.

"Nah, I'm good. I'm just slow is all." He gripped the frame of the cart and planted his fake leg on the ground first. Then his right leg. He stood up slowly. "Son, we have to tend to those brakes."

Chief Rand fist-pumped the air. "Let's go find that old tree."

We put on our backpacks and took off for the edge of the thick woods.

"The path should be right around here," Rand said as he scanned the border of the forest.

We followed along in the dusty road.

"Why are you looking up there?" I asked, confused.

Dad laughed. "Don't you remember? It's part of the riddle."

He got out the journal from his pack and thumbed through the weathered pages. "See, we have to follow the riddle in sections. Step by step. The first part says . . ." He read aloud the first lines.

> To find me you need to know
> X marks the spot is the way to go.
>
> Not on the ground. Near the sky!
> Find the tall ones who bend way up high.

We all craned our necks, looking for a supposed X . . . near the sky.

"What does that even mean, Dad?" I made sure to walk by his side just in case he lost his balance. Lucky trotted slightly ahead, but often looking back to check on Dad.

"I haven't the slightest clue," Dad said. "If it wasn't for Rand, honestly, I wouldn't even know where to begin." He looked around slowly, like he was soaking in the sights of the forest. "It's funny how he remembers so much of our childhood shenanigans. But one thing I do remember"—he took a big deep breath and released—"is how much I loved this place. I missed it." Dad looked at me and smiled. "It's great to be back. Hunting for the tree fort. With you."

I felt my chest expand and, in that moment, I felt I'd already found the best treasure of all. My dad was happy.

The forest was noisy with bird songs all around us. Some

birds were tucked in the shrubs. Others hovered and swooped above the treetops, snatching insects midflight. This place felt alive, when you took time to stop and get quiet. That's when the island's nature secrets came into focus.

"I'm glad you showed me my old journal." Dad patted me on the back as we walked slowly. "Rand and I had some good tales that I didn't write down, you know."

"Aww, you've got to tell me some."

He grinned and shook his head.

"Please . . . ," I begged.

"I'm sure you kids've got your own secret tales, too."

He wasn't wrong about that.

Rand walked closer, scratching his reddish beard. "If I remember correctly, the entrance is on the creekside. That way." Chief Rand waved his arm at the right side of the road.

"There it is!" Lovie's shout turned our attention toward where she pointed.

Two very tall palmettos leaned toward each other, with one trunk crossed in front of the other.

"I see it!" I shouted. "Way up there. The crossed trunks of the trees make a big X."

"Yes!" Lovie crossed her arms at the elbows to demonstrate.

"Good eye!" Macon called out.

"This way, kids," Chief Rand called out with a wave of his hand. "But watch your step. The grass is thick in here. And watch out for snakes."

We walked in single file through a thicket of short saw palmettos. It felt like walking through a hidden portal, but they could sure stick you. Chief Rank led and Dad brought up the rear. Well, actually, Lucky stayed at the end of the line, herding us. It was a narrow, beaten-down path, probably an animal trail. Chief Rand hiked through the understory of small shrubs, pushing away fallen limbs.

"Watch out for scat!" he yelled out.

Macon stopped to look closer at the animal droppings. "Raccoon poop," he called out.

How he knew that, I didn't want to ask. But I didn't doubt Macon was right. The path may have been easy for animals, but it wasn't so easy for us. Most especially my dad. Along with dodging branches and spiderwebs, we had to navigate our way around thorny vines and soft spots on the path. I knew these were serious obstacles for Dad.

I kept looking over my shoulder, checking on him. Mom had told me the thing Dad worried about most was falling. When we moved to Mount Pleasant, they bought a one-story house. It was easier and safer for him. One of my jobs at home was to keep the floors clear of everything that might trip Dad—shoes, socks, and even rugs. I was used to helping take care of my dad.

He was keeping up, but slowly. I saw the beads of sweat on his brow and the way he had to take care to gingerly move over the roots and stumps and everything else on the forest floor.

I was glad when Chief Rand stopped to take a break.

"Read the next clue, Eric," Chief Rand hollered out from the front of the pack.

Dad wiped his brow with his forearm and pulled the journal from his backpack. While we waited, we all took sips of water from our thermoses. It was hot and the no-see-ums were biting, but not as bad as the mosquitoes. It felt like we were in a jungle. I looked at Macon and Lovie. Their cheeks were pink from exertion, and they looked as tired as I was. I looked back at my dad, and my worry grew.

Dad found the page and began to read out loud.

Turn straight to the northern tide.
Then walk west because the tree must hide.

I saw Lovie's lips move as she repeated the riddle in her head.

"This way, adventurers!" Rand shouted from the front.

"Aye, aye!" Macon shouted back in a pirate voice.

"We're on a treasure hunt," Lovie sang loudly.

As the troop marched on, Dad was falling farther and farther behind. His shirt was soaked in sweat as he carefully placed each step. I stayed close to him, just like Lucky, and scouted out anything that might trip him.

"You know, Dad, this is our first hike together." I pushed through palmetto fronds and then held them back for Dad and Lucky to pass.

He winced and stopped, leaning his arm against a tree. "I

just need a short break." He rubbed his leg where his stump fit into the prosthesis.

"Sure." I tried not to show the worry that was creeping up inside me.

A strong breeze wafted through the woods, rattling palm fronds and shaking several pinecones loose from swaying longleaf pine trees. Dark clouds were coming in from over the ocean.

"Storm's coming," Dad said. "Maybe we should head back."

"But everyone's far ahead."

He turned to look at the way back, hands on his hips.

"Come on, Dad. We can catch up." I offered him my hand.

He brushed it away.

I swallowed hard, sensing the shift in his mood.

Dad took a deep breath, then said, "Let's go." He took a step forward. We began walking again, one slow step at a time. Lucky walked behind Dad on alert. He seemed more anxious than at the start of our hike. I continued keeping an eye out for stumps and pushed back branches that blocked our path. But I didn't notice the tangled thorny vine that caught Dad's leg at the ankle.

I heard my dad cry out and the sound of a loud thump on the ground.

"Dad!" I turned to see him lying on his side. Lucky was sniffing his neck. I hurried to his side. "Are you okay?"

He tightened his lips, not saying a word. I could see he was in pain.

"Can I get you something? Do you want me to get Chief Rand?"

"I don't need Rand," Dad growled out. In one swift move, he pulled out his pocketknife and cut the vine to free his foot.

Lucky nuzzled under Dad's arm, as if the dog thought he could help him back up.

Dad closed the pocketknife, stuffed it away, and then straightened both legs as he sat. Lucky sat beside him, watching him intently. I stayed silent as he sat and stared at his legs, panting hard to calm his breath.

"I'm done!" he shouted, punching the ground in frustration.

I drew back, my mouth dry.

He muttered a few harsh words to himself, then shook his head. "This is ridiculous. Who am I kidding? I *can't* do this!"

I didn't speak a word. I didn't know what to say. I was a little afraid.

We sat as a mockingbird called out in a nearby tree. Even Lucky rested on his haunches, as though waiting for a command. After a short while I heard a rustling from farther up along the path, and then Chief Rand burst out from the shrubs. My shoulders slumped with relief.

"I thought I lost y'all. Everything all right?" He looked at me and then to Dad. His expression shifted in understanding. Macon and Lovie caught up and peered at us from behind Chief Rand.

"What happened?" asked Macon.

I saw Lovie jab him in the ribs to be quiet.

"Nothing much," Dad said in an even voice. "I fell. I'm fine."

"It's tough hiking," Rand said in an encouraging tone. "The path is really overgrown up ahead. It's too tough for any of us to get through. I think we should head back. We need better tools to hack our way through that jungle."

"And more bug spray." Macon swatted his own neck.

Chief Rand bent to lend a hand to my dad. Wordlessly, my dad grabbed hold of Chief Rand's hand, and with one strong pull, he was back on his feet. He tottered a little to catch his balance, but I was relieved when he got steady on his feet. I hurried to pick up his backpack and handed it to him.

"Thanks," he said in a flat voice.

Thunder rumbled in the distance, low and ominous.

"Storm's a'coming, guys!" Macon pointed to dark clouds building overhead.

"It's so close I can smell it," Lovie said.

"It's coming in fast from the ocean. We'd better hustle. Let's go, Islanders!" Chief Rand stepped past Dad and once again led the pack along the worn path.

As we trudged back the way we came, the spark of excitement that I'd seen earlier in Dad's eyes had darkened, like the storm clouds that loomed over us.

To find me you need to know
X marks the spot is the way to go.

Not on the ground. Near the sky!
Find the tall ones who bend way up high.

Turn straight to the northern tide.
Then walk west because the tree must hide.

It's disguised as a huge beast
with big ogre feet and arms that stretch east.

Around her waist is a rope.
Use it to climb with strength and with hope.

Don't fear you're not strong enough.
Use the steps to climb all the way up.

Go where a wise owl might be.
There you'll find the treasure from the sea.

CHAPTER 11

A tropical depression

WE MADE IT TO OUR GOLF CARTS RIGHT as the clouds ripped open. Lightning flashed across the sky, and torrents of rain began to fall. The dirt road changed to a slippery mud track. I gripped the wheel tight, leaning far forward to see through the cloudy windshield.

"Hold tight!" I yelled over the drumbeat of rain beating on the roof of the cart. "I can hardly see."

I took it slow. Driving a cart during a downpour was like driving in Jell-O. The road jiggled and swished around us. I dropped off Lovie first, then Macon. By the time I pulled into the open-air garage beneath Honey's house, I was drenched and my hands hurt from gripping the steering wheel. I slowly flexed all ten fingers with a new understanding of the expression "white-knuckled ride."

Lightning crackled in the sky again, and I counted only to three before thunder clapped so loud it vibrated through my body. I ducked to the ground out of sheer reflex. A minute later, the headlights of Dad's cart cut through the sheets of rain as it rocked and swayed up the rutted driveway. Chief Rand was in the driver's seat this time. Dad was holding tight to Lucky. For the dog's safety or his own comfort . . . maybe both.

"Nice little summer storm we got." Chief Rand stood up. Leaves were stuck to his face and hair. Mud streaked his left side.

"Little?" I shouted over the downpour. I waddled over to Dad, feeling like a penguin in my soggy underwear. "Are you sure this isn't a hurricane?"

Another powerful thunder boom, seemingly right overhead, made us all freeze for a moment. The chief walked over to me and leaned closer.

"You can't ride the elevator during a storm. You have to wait."

My heart sank. This would really add to my dad's frustration. I nodded with understanding.

The house lights flickered a few times. Honey brought us cups of hot tea with honey and milk. "To warm up your insides," she said.

We all sat under the house in silence, watching the storm winds sway the trees and hoping the power would stay on. It did, thankfully. Later, when the storm was over, Dad was able to ride the lift up to the house. He retreated to his room, with Lucky following behind.

Summer storms on the Carolina coast usually don't last long, but this was a tropical depression that hovered over the island for the next three days. The rain kept us all cooped up inside. We were starting to get on each other's nerves. Dad was back to being distant. He didn't talk about the tree fort hunt. He didn't really talk about anything. He kept his comments short and instead filled the days with reading. Dad's favorite place to sit was the dining table. I knew that the firm wooden, wide-legged chairs and table gave him stability. Plus it was close to all the things he needed—the fridge, bedroom, and bathroom.

I lay on the floor petting Lucky when I saw Honey carry a cup of tea to my dad.

"You might try working on your nature journal. That always used to entertain you when you were a boy," Honey suggested.

"Maybe later," Dad replied, not looking up from his book.

Honey took a deep breath and walked back into the kitchen. I heard the pots and pans banging. I wanted to shout that I was as sick and tired of tiptoeing around my dad as she was. And I was dying of boredom being stuck inside. For the first time since I'd arrived, I wanted to binge-watch videos and TV shows, or at least download a computer game.

I rose and went over to Honey's laptop. A world of fun was a click away. I plopped down on the chair and called out, "*Please* . . . can I play on the computer, just this one day?"

Honey walked around the counter from the kitchen, drying her hands on a towel, to stand beside me. "You know that's not going to happen. Why don't you read a book, like your father?"

I slumped and put my chin in my palm. "I'm not in the mood."

"Why not call Macon?"

"He's busy with his sister."

"What about Lovie?"

"She has to stay home on Isle of Palms, on account of the rain." Each time I spoke, it sounded like a moan.

I could tell Honey was trying to be cheerful. "Why not play a game with your father? Monopoly. Or cards."

I frowned and felt my frustration simmer. "He won't," I grumbled.

Honey clasped her hands in front of her and turned her head toward my dad. "I see." She released a long sigh of pent-up air. "I suppose you could go online. To work on your journal," she added when I jerked my head up. She said that in the tone that let me know she was doing me a big favor. "Is there something you'd like to research?"

The only time I could go online was if I needed to find

facts and learn something new. Usually for my journal. Even then, an hour a day was the limit. Maybe it was the weather. Maybe it was my dad ignoring me. Or maybe it was being cooped up for days, but suddenly, I was mad. I slammed my palm down on the table. "I just want to play a video game!"

Honey sucked in her breath, shocked at my outburst. I paled, knowing I'd overstepped my bounds. Lucky sprang to his feet. Even my dad turned from his book to check what was going on.

Honey squared her shoulders and looked me straight in the eyes. Her own were bright with anger. "Jake, you're not a little child. You're twelve years old. And, you!" She turned to face my dad and said accusingly, "You're forty. You're both acting like spoiled children. I've heard enough of your bellyaching. Find something to do. I'm getting a change of scenery. You can find me at the Nature Center. Call me if you need me!" she announced before storming out the door.

I needed to get out of the house too. Before Dad could say anything, I raced to grab my raincoat from the hooks by the door. "Hey, boy!" I called out to Lucky in a super-happy voice. "Want to go for a walk?" I grabbed his leash off the wall hook. Judging by how fast he got to his feet, yep, even the dog needed an escape.

I got a lucky break when I saw the rain had stopped. If only temporarily. I drove straight to Macon's house.

"You saved me, bro!" Macon said as he climbed onto the right side of the cart, sandwiching Lucky between us. "I was going nuts being my baby sister's entertainer." He flopped his head back. "Babies are exhausting!" When he straightened, he turned to me and asked, "Where are we going?"

"Does it matter?"

Macon laughed and shook his head. "Just go!"

We drove around in the drizzle for a while, splashing through muddy sections of the main paths. When I drove through a hole that was deeper than I expected, the cart's wheel jerked and slung mud up onto the windshield.

"That was a close call," I said, gripping the wheel tight. "Honey will kill me if I wreck this cart. What should we do now? There is no way I can go home right now."

"Same here," Macon responded. His arm draped around Lucky. "I know. The Huyler House." He pointed at the small wooden road sign ahead. "I'll battle you in Ping-Pong or foosball. And we'll stay dry."

"Say no more. Hold on tight," I yelled, taking a sharp right turn into the parking lot.

As soon as we got near the screen door entrance, Macon stopped in his tracks, making me almost crash right into him. "Shh!" He swung around. "This is not good."

I peered over his shoulder. Eddie and Andy were playing a game of pool. I groaned. "Not. Them," I said through gritted teeth. "Let's go." I turned on my heel to sneak away, but Macon grabbed my arm.

"We can't slink away now. If those dingbats see us, they'll think we're scared of them."

Macon squared his shoulders; his decision was made. "There's no turning back now. You go first."

I walked in first, holding Lucky's leash. The Island Invaders looked up as we approached. Their surprise shifted to sneers.

"What's up, nature geeks?" Eddie said. Andy was leaning over a pool table, concentrating on his next shot.

Smack!

Andy hit the black eight ball into a corner pocket. "I win!" he gloated.

"Whatever. Beginner's luck," Eddie said, and then held his pool cue out like a sword toward Andy. "On guard!"

I watched as they both began play-fighting like pirates, jumping up on chairs and picnic tables, and running around.

"They are the definition of obnoxious," Macon said, tossing me one of the paddles from the Ping-Pong table. "Prepare to battle!"

I was rusty at the game, but I still managed to hold my own. We were tied at ten to ten, Macon's serve, when the screen door squeaked open.

"Hey, guys!" said a familiar voice behind me.

Eddie and Andy, who were now making light-saber sounds while whacking at each other's pool cues, froze in mid-battle. As I turned my head, Lovie was standing behind me with a book tucked under her arm.

Whack! Bounce!

Macon served the ball when I wasn't looking. "Score! I win!" He celebrated with a little dance over to Lovie, pretending to give her an over-the-head, double-handed high five.

"Okaaay . . . ," Lovie said slowly.

"Cheater," I teased Macon. "I wasn't even looking."

"Never take your eye off the ball. Sorry, dude." He turned to me, offering a fist bump. "Good game, though."

Lovie twirled her braid in one hand, not saying anything. I didn't know what to say either, which made everything feel awkward. Lucky broke the ice as he jumped up on Lovie with his front two paws, making her stumble back slightly.

"Aww! Hey, Lucky!" she said, running her hand down his furry brown ears and head. Macon joined Lovie to pet Lucky, who now flopped to his side for a belly rub.

"What are you doing here?" he asked Lovie. "I thought the storm kept you at home."

"I was just about to ask you guys the same thing," Lovie replied, glancing up at me. "Were y'all looking for me?"

"No," I replied, grabbing Lucky's leash from the floor. "Were you looking for us?"

She paused for a moment. "Nope," she replied. I detected annoyance in her voice.

Eddie sauntered over to Lovie and threw his arm over her shoulder with a big grin. "Hey, turtle girl! Where ya been?"

So, it was back to that. Now I really wanted to leave. "Let's go, Macon." I tugged at Lucky's leash as I walked toward the screen door.

"Where are you going?" asked Lovie. Her tone sounded hurt.

Eddie stood beside her with this smug grin on his face.

"Out," I said. I didn't realize how much I just sounded like my dad.

That night Macon and I made plans to have our first sleepover. I had wanted to stay at his house because he had a gaming system, but he refused, saying that we'd have to be too quiet when his sister went to bed, and then she'd be waking the entire house up. "She still doesn't sleep through the night," he warned.

So I gave in and said we'd have the sleepover at my place.

"Every time I come up here, I think this place is AM-MA-ZING!" Macon said when he reached the top step of the ladder to my room.

"Thanks. I like it. But I hope you don't mind that it's missing one entire wall."

Macon set down his hiking backpack and leaned over the railing. All quiet below. Dad and Honey went to bed early most nights, so we'd be able to hang out in my loft or the living room without anyone bothering us.

Macon ran over to my massive round window. "Dude! This feels like some crazy cool portal to another world."

I smiled, glad to know he thought this loft was as cool as I did.

He pulled out his camping mattress, which he blew up in seconds with a handheld air pump. Then he unrolled an orange sleeping bag, a tiny foam pillow, a head lamp, a first-aid kit, water bottle, pocketknife, a Ziploc bag of toiletries, a compass, and snacks.

"You're just staying over one night, you know," I teased.

"It's my camping gear from Boy Scouts. Tonight's a good excuse to use it."

"If I had known you had all this, we could have organized a campout, not a sleepover!"

"Yeah, if only it'd just stop raining," Macon added. We both looked over at the big window, covered in raindrops.

I laid out the snacks from Honey. Since it was a special night having a friend over, Honey had prepared a big bowl of popcorn.

"This is better than at the movie theater!" Macon declared, popping another handful into his mouth

Honey had also pulled out her old board games. We picked out Battleship first. Macon won. Then checkers. Macon won that too. And then my favorite—Monopoly.

As we played and snacked, Macon and I talked and talked. It felt good to share all the thoughts that were running through our heads.

"My sister is driving me crazy," Macon said as he rolled the dice. "I mean, she's always crying. And if she isn't crying, she's pooping." He moved his piece seven spaces. "Seems all my mama does anymore is change her diapers, or feed her, or play with her. It's like she doesn't even know I'm alive, except when she needs me to help with my sister."

I took my turn. "You think that's bad? My dad sulks around

the house all day. He won't play games. He won't talk about the tree fort. Heck, he doesn't talk to me at all. And he's not a baby. What's his excuse?"

Macon bent to roll the dice. "He lost his leg, man. That's got to be hard. And the whole going to war and all. Pretty major."

He was right, but that didn't make me feel any better. I watched him move his game piece three spaces, then fist-pump. "Boardwalk. Buy it!"

"At least your sister isn't making your life miserable on purpose. She's just being a baby."

"I don't think your dad is making your life miserable on purpose," Macon said, leaning over to grab the Boardwalk card.

I rolled the dice. "Sure feels like it sometimes. Last year, all I thought about was how much I missed my dad. I couldn't wait to spend this summer with him here on Dewees. And now . . ." I threw the dice. "Sometimes I wish he wasn't here."

We both stared at the snake eyes on the dice, but neither of us moved.

"I get it," Macon said. "Last summer all I wanted was to be a big brother. And now that I am, I wish my sister would, I don't know . . . go away."

Neither of us spoke for a moment.

"Stalemate," I said, yawning. "This game could go on for days. Let's turn in."

Macon stretched and yawned. "Yeah."

I climbed onto my bed while Macon lay down on his air mattress and slid into his sleeping bag next to me on the floor. We lay on our backs and stared out the big portal window. Usually, I'd see countless bright stars flickering in the sky. But not tonight. Instead, we listened to the faint rumbles of thunder and watched silent strobes of lightning flicker. In the darkness, I felt I could speak about things I couldn't when the lights were on.

"You awake?"

"Yeah." Macon's voice sounded far away.

"Why do you think Lovie is acting so weird this summer?" I asked Macon.

"Duh. She likes you."

I sat up, wide awake. "What? No way!"

"Way," he replied in a low voice. "Lovie likes you."

"Sure. We're friends."

"No, I mean, really likes you. Emoji heart eyes level, dude."

"What? She does not," I replied, feeling my cheeks flame at the thought. I was glad for the dark. I lay down on my back. "You really think Lovie *likes me* likes me?"

"Yep."

I wondered if I could believe him. I was almost afraid to think it was true.

Then he asked, "Do you like her back?"

I didn't respond immediately. The thought of a pretty girl having a crush on you is cool. But this was not just a girl. It was Lovie Legare. My friend. *Our* friend. One of *The Islanders*.

"No. She's our friend. That's it," I answered with a bit of heat.

"Okay." Macon didn't seem convinced. "Speaking of friends . . . she's hanging out an awful lot with those Invaders. I feel like she's betraying us with Eddie and Andy."

I'd thought the same thing but felt I had to stick up for Lovie. "No, I think she's just being, you know, Lovie. Nice to everyone." At least that's what I hoped. I pushed back the image of seeing Eddie put his arm around our friend. Then I remembered the way she sounded when we said we were leaving without her.

"Maybe we *are* leaving her out. A bit."

"Well, can you blame us? I feel like she's always with those other guys this summer. She better not invite them to join the treasure hunt."

"No," I agreed. "Our mission is to find that treasure this summer. If she wants part of it, she'll have to join us. Not them."

"Yeah," Macon agreed on another yawn. Then he was quiet.

My eyes got heavy as I thought about Lovie. I wondered if she really did like me in that way. Or if the person she liked was Eddie.

Or if it mattered at all. I just wanted my friend back.

CHAPTER 12

Seek and ye shall find

HONEY WOKE US UP WITH A HOT BREAKFAST of cheesy grits and bacon. Then, after our bellies were full, she rushed us out the door to take care of chores.

"I have a grocery delivery arriving at the ferry landing at nine-thirty this morning. You can't be late," she warned. "And there's Neapolitan ice cream in that order."

"Got it! We'll be speedy," I said as I headed for the door.

"Always protect the ice cream," Macon said, making Honey laugh.

Macon helped me load up the golf cart with the garbage and recyclables before we headed over to the dump site, which was right next to the island fire station. We looked for Chief Rand as we drove by, but there were two younger firefighters on duty. We still waved hello.

Macon poured all the recycled items into an enormous blue bin and grimaced. "So noisy!"

I carried a smelly, heavy trash bag in one hand to the nearby metal bin with the word GARBAGE spray-painted in stenciled lettering. I sucked in a big lungful of air, holding my breath for the toss and run. With my free hand, I lifted the black plastic lid. Just as I released the bag onto the heap of other bags, out popped a raccoon head.

I yelled and jumped back, throwing my fists up. At the same moment, the furry masked bandit hissed at me and jumped out, tumbling to the ground. Then, without a backward glance, it darted off. I held a fighter stance as I watched the raccoon's bushy black-and-gray striped tail disappear beneath some bushes.

"You should have seen your face." Macon howled with laughter. "And why are you standing like that? Were you gonna punch a scared little raccoon?"

I suddenly realized how ridiculous I looked and lowered my fists, but I was still on high alert.

"Dude! I think I know what a heart attack must feel like." I pressed one of my hands to my chest. Macon just kept on belly-laughing.

"It popped up faster than a whack-a-mole game! I thought that thing was going to jump on me!"

"This moment is totally going in my nature journal!" Macon said. "Beware of dumpster-diving raccoons!"

I gave him a playful jab. "Come on, let's go. The boatload of groceries is going to be here soon."

As we hopped back on the cart, he looked at me, shook his head, and chuckled one last time.

"I can't believe you were scared of a cute little raccoon."

"I wasn't scared. Just caught off guard," I defended myself.

"Uh-huh. Sure."

When Macon wasn't looking, I took a final glance behind me. That raccoon had me feeling jumpy now.

There was no mail for Honey at the mailbox, so we hung around the dock waiting for the ferry. The sea was steely gray, matching the sky above. Looking at the choppy water, I thought the ferry might be late. I tucked my hands in my pockets and walked aimlessly down the dock. I was still bored, but being bored outdoors felt better than being bored inside four walls. There was always something different to look at outside, some fish or bird or critter popping up to surprise you.

I bent over the dock's railing and, sure enough, I got my surprise. There was Lovie down on the floating platform. She was alone, searching around along the water's edge for something.

"Lovie!" I shouted. She turned, and seeing me, waved and ran up to join us. I hurried up the dock to the covered area where Macon was reading the bulletin board.

"Look who's here," he said in a friendly way when Lovie trotted near.

"Hey, guys," she said. "Long time no see."

"Did you lose something?" I asked her.

She twisted her lips in confusion. "Sort of, I guess. Come look, you guys."

Curious, we followed her down the metal plank to the lower platform. It was low tide and the shallow water lapped against the exposed chocolaty mud flats, dotted with fiddler crab holes. We peered over the edge.

"What are we looking for?" Macon asked.

"Well, yesterday I took Eddie and Andy around to look for scavenger hunt items," she said.

"Scavenger hunt?" I asked, confused.

"Are you talking about the geocache course that's posted on the board at the Nature Center?" Macon asked.

"Oh, that," I said, understanding what she meant. Honey had been excited by our treasure hunt and created a kind of scavenger hunt of her own. It was called a geocache and to find treasures, or cache, you had to use maps, geography clues, and GPS.

"Honey just finished setting up the course," I said. "She won't be happy if one of her stations is missing already."

Lovie grimaced. "I know," she said as she slowly pulled up a rope that was tied to the dock. I could see that the other end of the rope was frayed.

"Somebody cut it," Macon said in a shocked voice.

"I was really excited to play the game. We used the GPS on our phones, and I helped them find the first two geo-cache locations. I got a compass in one. They didn't want that. I left a bird feather in the container. There was a key chain in the second one, and Andy took that. I was annoyed that he didn't leave anything behind. That's a big rule of the hunt. If you take something, you have to leave something. So I put my compass back in the second one. Andy is so annoying," she said, frowning. "Then it started to rain again, so we all raced home."

She plopped the rope back into the water. "I forgot to put one of the clues back into its geocache container. So today I came back here to return it. But the geocache is gone!"

"I bet I can guess exactly what happened," I said. "Those two Invaders are always doing bonehead things."

Lovie stared at me in shock. "You think they came out here and just took it?" she asked, scrunching up her nose in disgust. "Really?"

Macon nodded. "They've been nothing but creeps since they got here."

"I don't want to think that. That's just . . . beyond awful."

"Do you have any other ideas?" Macon asked.

"We can't figure out why you're hanging out with them. Especially after the slingshot," I said, surprised at how mad I was feeling.

"I'm just trying to be nice."

"Maybe it's time to not be so nice to them," I said.

"Maybe." Lovie frowned with a sigh. "Yeah." Then she tilted her head with curiosity, eyeing us up and down. "Um, are you guys wearing *pajamas?*"

Wearing my pajamas while doing chores seemed like a fun idea earlier. But now, seeing the way Lovie was looking at me like she was about to burst out laughing, I suddenly wished I could crawl into one of those mud holes along the bank.

"Oh, yeah!" Macon said, totally not caring that we were in our pjs. "We had a sleepover. At Jake's."

Lovie's smile fell. "A sleepover? Why wasn't I invited?"

"Well, no offense," I said, not wanting to make eye contact. "You know . . . you're a girl."

"Well, fine." She crossed her arms. "You could have at least invited me to hang out."

I slipped my hands in my pockets and looked away.

Lovie shot her nose up slightly. "I see you guys already have plans. That don't include me." She eyed our pajamas one more time, making me feel even more self-conscious, before walking back up the boat ramp. "Your shirt's on backward," she called back without turning.

I looked down slowly. She was right. A swirl of embarrassment and sadness rose in my mind as I watched her walk away, her long braid bouncing against her back.

"Sheesh," Macon said. "She's got that nose so high in the air, if it was still raining, she'd drown."

"Cut it out," I snapped. "I feel bad. She's our friend."

"You're right. I didn't mean to talk bad about your girlfriend!" Macon slapped me on my back, laughing.

I glared at him.

"Lighten up. I was just teasing."

I returned home with the groceries before the next bout of rain began to fall. Lucky barked and jumped when I walked into the house. The best part of having a dog was he was always happy to see me. As I pet him, I looked around the house. I didn't see Dad, but Honey was sitting at the computer. She was so deep in thought, she didn't hear me come in.

"Hey, Honey. What are you doing?" I asked when I reached her side.

Honey startled, bringing her hands to her chest. "You gave me a fright! I didn't hear you come in."

"What are you doing?" I asked again.

She looked at me in her matter-of-fact way. "I'm making sure that no mud or weeds or brambles ruin my grandson's dream of finding a treasure."

I smiled, liking the sound of that. "How are you doing that?"

"Well, sir," she began, turning back to the computer. She began pecking away on the keyboard, then paused and tapped the screen. "Every mission needs proper supplies." She squinted at the screen. "So, tell me, Jake, for your expedition, what do you need?"

I leaned against the chair, warming to the task. I thought of the hard hike through the brush, and my answer came readily. "Definitely a hatchet, to whack back the vines."

She nodded and typed in my request. "We're in luck," she said readjusting her glasses. "Says right here they have a camping hatchet available. That should do the trick." She looked me in the eye. "We'll let Rand handle that item, right?"

"Yeah, of course," I said, but I was disappointed. One of my favorite books was *Hatchet*, and I dreamed of surviving alone in the wilderness like Brian.

Honey clicked. "Now, what else?"

"Um, how about a chainsaw, in case of fallen logs?"

She gave me the kind of look that only grown-ups give kids. "Absolutely not, Jake Potter." Shifting back to the shopping screen, she said, "I was thinking rubber boots. Everybody needs a pair." Honey eyeballed my bare feet. "What's your shoe size now?"

I gave her my size and then, thinking of feet, I said, "But what about Dad?"

"Oh, I'll get him a pair too. I think he can slip it on over his prosthetic, same as you and me."

"No, what I meant was . . . what if he can't make it through the woods? It's a long way to the tree fort." I paused, not wanting to betray my dad, but I felt she had to know. "He had a real hard time keeping up," I told her in a whisper.

Honey waved her hand in dismissal. "You don't have to whisper. Rand came by and dragged him out to the firehouse. Thank the Lord."

"Pluff mud stole my shoes last summer, remember?" I con-

tinued. "What if he gets stuck in a muddy spot and loses ..." I paused. "You know."

Honey paused in thought, tapping the pad of her index finger on her lip. "Do you still have that island map handy?"

I rushed over to the ladder, Lucky at my feet, barking. I climbed up to the loft and went straight to my backpack, found the map, then raced back to Honey. She spread it out on the desk, and I pointed out the area where we had hiked.

"Dad and Chief Rand think the tree is close to the water."

"The water, eh?" Honey studied the map for a long moment. "I wonder," she muttered, and ran her finger from a floating dock on the back side of the island, then along a creek that wound its way like a snake in the marsh grass right to a spot near where we'd hiked. Her eyes twinkled, and she clapped her hands together with excitement. "By golly! Seek and ye shall find. Unless I'm mistaken, and when it comes to Dewees, I rarely am, you can get there by kayak!"

We shared a look of understanding. Then I released a whoop so loud, it sent Lucky barking all over again.

Honey laughed and hugged me close. "Child, I do believe your joy cry will chase those dark clouds clear away!"

CHAPTER 13

One thing about The Islanders: We work well as a team

THE NEXT MORNING, THE SUN PEEKED OUT from the clouds and poured its bright light through my window right to my eyes, as if to say, *Rise and shine!* I popped out of bed, charged up for my new mission. I just needed to convince my friends to help.

It was great to feel the sun shining again. As I drove along the familiar road, it cheered me up to see the blue sky and white clouds. It seemed to me that the trees and shrubs looked greener than ever after a good watering. In fact, they were soaked. Every time the wind blew, droplets of water sprinkled from the leaves. The road had big puddles I had to navigate around, and here and there I spotted a fallen limb. Soon enough all would be dry.

Even the birds were enjoying the sun. When I passed the pond, I spotted a pair of anhingas standing still, beaks pointed skyward, their black wings spread out to dry. Honey taught me that anhingas were different from most water birds. They didn't have oil glands to waterproof their wings. After they dove for fish, they had to dry their feathers.

First, I went to the beach access that led to our gazebo. I saw Lovie's cart and was glad I didn't miss her. I glanced at my watch. It was seven a.m. Prompt as ever, Lovie came walking up from the beach in her Turtle Team T-shirt and cutoff jeans. She smiled when she spied me waiting, and seeing it, I smiled back, relieved. I guess that meant she wasn't mad anymore.

"How did you know I was here?" she asked.

"Turtle Patrol," I replied. Lovie continued to help the island Turtle Team long after our community service last summer.

"Duh, of course. It was a great morning, too!" I enjoyed listening to her as we walked side by side back up the boardwalk toward the golf carts.

"I found the big loggerhead tracks," Lovie said, her hands moving in the air to show how large the tracks were. "We've got another nest. That's twelve nests so far this season. Ms. Alicia and Ms. Judy were out there with me and said they'd never had such a good year." She looked down almost shyly when she added, "They called me their good luck charm."

"That's really great," I told her, and she seemed pleased to hear my enthusiasm. "Makes me miss Dawn Patrol. Almost."

She laughed. "You should come out with Honey some morning." She spun on her heel to face me as she talked. "And I found all these little, teeny-tiny turtle tracks in the sand. They were toy-sized. So cute," she cooed. "Judy counted at least eighty of them, and they were all heading in the right direction, straight for the ocean."

"Did you see any baby turtles?"

"Hatchlings? No. But that's a good thing. That means they all made it to the water."

Honey had told me that when the hatchlings finally dug out from deep in the nest, their instinct told them to head toward the brightest light. In nature, that was the moon and stars over the ocean. I remembered all the nights I'd stared at the bright moon and stars overhead, sometimes so bright the moon was like a spotlight from heaven. But with all the rain lately, and the moon covered up with clouds, Honey was worried lights from the houses would shine so bright the hatchlings would turn around and follow the artificial light. To their death.

"They only have about three days of food stored up to make it to the ocean and to swim all the way to the Gulf Stream," Lovie told me.

"Where'd you learn all this?"

"From the team," she said with pride. "They're teaching me so I can be an official member of the team when I get older."

"That's cool."

"You can be a team member too."

"Maybe I will."

"So," Lovie began again, "in three days the team will open up the nest to check and see how many eggs hatched. There might even be a poor little hatchling that couldn't get out."

"I'd like to see that."

Lovie looked toward the sea. "We could go together."

"Uh, sure." Our eyes met and we both smiled and looked away.

We started walking toward our golf carts in silence. I reached my cart when I remembered why I'd come to see her in the first place.

"Hey, Lovie," I called.

She was sitting in her cart, adjusting her seat belt. She looked up and smiled again. "Yes?"

"I need your help today."

"Sure. What do you need?"

"Honey and I have a plan. She figured out that we can reach the area of the tree fort by water. So, first we need to help get my dad out in a kayak," I explained.

"Doesn't he know how to kayak already?"

"Yes, but he hasn't been kayaking as an amputee. He gets nervous about doing new things. Anyway, I'm thinking if *all* of us go out in kayaks, it'll be fun and he won't feel so self-conscious."

"And if he does go kayaking, it will help get us one step closer to finding that tree fort."

"Right," I said. "And the treasure map."

"Name the place and the time!" Lovie called, and turned on her cart.

I gave her a thumbs-up and took off to find Macon.

With all three friends in agreement, it was time to get to work cleaning the kayaks. Outside at the Bird's Nest, Lovie was filling up a bucket with soapy water while Macon helped me get down Honey's old kayaks. They were covered in sand, dirt, leaves, and we were afraid to find out what else. The underbelly of the house wasn't a closed garage like my parents had in Mount Pleasant. It was open to the wind, rain, and wild. And with a dirt floor, everything needed a good cleaning now and then. My chores included raking the leaves and sand out of the space, but it was like trying to keep back an ocean wave with your palm. The dirt and sand kept blowing in.

Macon and I were pulling down the last kayak when a small green tree frog leaped out of the kayak's hole right onto Macon's shirt!

His eyes bugged out, and he dropped the kayak, flailing his arms, jumping, and screeching, "Get it off! Get it off!"

The tiny green frog, no bigger than an inch, clung to his T-shirt.

I doubled over in laughter. I knew I shouldn't laugh, but I couldn't help it.

Lovie had the water hose in her hand and, in a smooth move, aimed the stream at Macon, drenching him.

Macon screamed again, this time from the surprise of being squirted with cold water. It was over quick. He stood stock-still and dripping wet with his eyes squeezed shut.

"Is . . . it still there?"

"It's gone, bro. You're totally fine," I said, trying not to laugh again.

Macon opened his eyes and slowly looked down at his chest, his face etched with fear. He brought his hand to his chest, and finding nothing there, slumped with relief.

I sucked in a big breath, trying to hold in another laugh. "That might have been the funniest thing I've seen. I mean ever!" I couldn't help it. I started laughing again.

Lovie burst out laughing too, covering her mouth as though trying to stop it.

"Ha. Ha. Totally not funny!" Macon said, shaking the water off his face and hair. "Thanks for nothing," he said to me.

"It was just a harmless little tree frog," said Lovie. "Probably the cutest frog on the entire island."

"Yeah, they're cute when they're sitting still on some tree out in the wild!" he said. His voice was higher than normal. "It attacked me!"

"Attacked you?" Lovie laughed again. "You mean *jumped* on you."

"Easy for you to say," Macon said with a scowl, and tried to dry his face with his wet T-shirt. "Stop laughing!"

"Remember when you laughed at me about the raccoon?" I said, trying to stop my laughter. "Now we're even." I went to the kayak, getting really close, and searched the ground near it. "There it is," I said, crouching low. "It's, like, the length of my pinkie."

The frog gave out a throaty squeak before hopping to the camouflaged safety of a nearby bush.

"So ferocious," I teased. "And by the way, I'm writing this frog moment down in my nature journal!"

Macon smirked, then let out a short laugh. "Whatever."

I walked to the kayak and bent to pick up the front. "Come on, let's get back to work."

One thing about The Islanders: We work well as a team. We grabbed rags and began washing years of dirt and pollen, clumps of leaves, and even some cobwebs off the three kayaks, and when we were done, we began work on the stand-up paddleboard, paddles, and life jackets. We laid everything out in the sun to dry and stepped back to admire our work. I was feeling pretty good, until I felt the smack of a sloppy rag hit my back.

I spun around to face Macon, my rag ready to be fired, but saw he was standing with his rag in his hand without a clue. Confused, I slowly turned toward Lovie when—*ouch!* I felt the sting of a taut rag snapped against my thigh. I spun to see

Lovie crouched in the ready, with another rag hanging from her hand and mischief in her eyes.

With a howl, I launched my soapy rag. She squealed and ducked, then spun around and fired her rag at me. This time she missed. Laughing, I ran for the wet rag lying on the ground. I bent to grab it and—*snap!* I felt another shot hit me in the rear.

"Perfect target!" called out Macon, laughing.

It was on! Rags were flying as we ducked, tossed, and dipped our rags into the soapy water. At some point we all just stopped, tired, panting, and dripping soapy, dirty water from head to toe. We looked at each other and burst out laughing. We laughed so hard we were doubled over, holding on to our stomachs. It hurt in a good way. After all those days of rain and gloom and arguments, this is what I missed most about being with Macon and Lovie. We could just be us and have fun.

I figured it would take a little convincing to get my dad on board with Honey's plan, especially since he had been in a funk since our last outing. Macon and Lovie went home while I planned out what to say. I ran up the stairs to change, pumped that at least the kayaks were ready.

Dad was sitting on the sofa with Lucky at his feet. He was writing in his new journal—a good sign.

"Doing your summer homework?"

"I'm giving it a good attempt." He finished writing, then

looked up at me. "What was all that screaming outside earlier? And why are you soaked to your skin?"

"It's a great story, Dad, but I'll tell you all about it later. I need to dry off." I left a dripping trail across Honey's clean floor as I headed to the bathroom for a towel and then climbed the ladder to the loft to change into dry clothes. I grabbed Dad's old journal and headed back downstairs. I took a seat across from him.

He lowered his pen and looked at me, curiosity sparking in his blue eyes. "I'm all ears."

"Okay," I began in earnest. "I have a great idea. I want you to hear me out, okay? And please say yes."

He clicked the tip of his pen and closed his notebook. "You've got my attention."

I took a deep breath and told him about everything Honey and I had studied on the island map, and about Honey's genius idea to reach the tree fort by water.

"We can get around to the tree by kayak." I held my breath.

Dad's brows flew up to the top of his forehead. I rushed to continue before he could say no.

"Remember how much you used to love canoeing and kay-aking? Well, that screaming you heard was Lovie, Macon, and me cleaning the kayaks up. For you."

Dad tilted his head. "For me?"

"Yes. See, after Honey's great idea, we researched kayaking as, well . . ."—I stumbled on the word—"an amputee." It was a word that felt new on my lips.

His expression shifted, but I couldn't tell if that was a good thing, so I continued. "Dad, you can do this. *We* can do this. *Together.* This is totally the way to get to the tree. We've got it all figured out, and with the clues in your riddle . . ."

Dad put his hand up, a cue for me to pause. He closed his eyes for a moment, taking two deep breaths before answering me.

"Jake, I absolutely love your enthusiasm. I really do, but . . ."

My heart plummeted to the floor at that final word. *But.* That one word was always the beginning of an excuse. He looked away, thinking about what to say next.

"Please . . . ," I begged. "Even Macon's agreed to kayak. And he's never done it. We could all do a practice together."

"No."

The word stung. "What do you mean? Why?"

"I'm sorry, but my answer is no."

I felt heat climb my neck. "I don't understand, Dad," I said, hearing the pleading in my voice. "It'll be fun. We'll help you." When he looked away, I blurted out, "You can't say no."

"I *can't* do it!" he roared.

I felt the blood drain from my face. His booming voice jolted Lucky from his nap and right to his feet.

Dad put his fingers to the bridge of his nose and took a deep breath. When he spoke again, his voice was low, but it trembled, like he was trying hard to control the emotions choking him.

"Nothing is easy for me, Jake! Don't you get it? Everything. Every. Single. Thing is hard."

The heat on my neck reached my eyes, and I fought back hot tears.

"I can't take a hike in the woods. I can't hop in a kayak with you. Or climb a tree. Or walk the beach. Or go anywhere else with you on this stupid treasure hunt. So just drop it." He planted his feet and pushed off the couch to stand.

I felt my words mingle with my frustration and hurt and anger until it felt like boiling lava in my throat about to erupt. I leaped to my feet and looked at his retreating back.

"Liar!" I shouted at him.

My dad stopped walking and stood very still. Then he slowly turned to face me. His face was taut with anger. "What did you call me?"

I didn't back down. I had a summer's worth of frustration bubbling in my veins.

"You always told me to never give up. To always try. To face my fears." I could feel tears wet my cheeks, and I struggled to get my words out through my trembling lips. "But look at you. You're being a hypocrite. You're giving up! Not just on the treasure hunt or going kayaking. But everything!" I swallowed hard. "You're giving up on being my dad."

The tears blurred my vision as I looked down at his old leather journal. Suddenly everything felt like such a waste of time. I grabbed it from the couch and hurled it across the room. It landed with a dull thud.

Dad didn't move. He didn't speak.

I swiped my eyes with the back of my arm. "Forget it. I

don't want to do this stupid treasure hunt anymore. I give up too. Just like you."

I jerked my backpack onto my shoulder and blew out of the house with the force of the storm that had just swept across our island.

"Jake!" I heard him yell just as I slammed the door. I didn't want to hear anything more.

I hid from the world at the top of a wooden two-story lookout tower, one of several on the island. I tucked my legs close to my chest and looked out over the creek and grass that created a patchwork quilt of blue and green below me. As I watched a flock of pelicans fly in formation over the water, I wished I had their freedom to just flap my wings and go as I pleased. No rules, no arguments. Just flying free in the open sky.

It was my stomach that forced me down from my refuge. That and the bug bites. I wondered if it was possible to be eaten alive by no-see-ums and mosquitoes. The sky had shifted to the yellow, orange, and red of sunset. But I didn't want to go home. I wished I could go to Macon's house because I could tell him just about everything. But not this. This was between me and my dad.

Honey welcomed me home with relief and tears shining in her eyes. "Are you hungry?"

I nodded.

"You missed dinner, not that it was much. Meat loaf. I made you a sandwich. I figured you'd be hungry."

"Thanks." She handed me a plate, and I carried it to the table. Sheepishly, I glanced over to the living room. Dad was sitting on the sofa with his back to me. He was giving me the silent treatment. Not that it mattered, because I wasn't in the mood to talk anyway.

"Can I take it up to the loft?" I asked Honey.

Honey reached out to run her fingers in my hair. "Sure you can. Good night, dear boy."

I retreated from the silent war to my loft.

I scarfed down my sandwich, then climbed into bed. I tried to read, but I couldn't get into any story. So I gave up and clicked off my lamp. Here's the thing about sleeping in a loft. There isn't a door you can close to shut out the noise. There isn't even a wall. Every sound floats up to my loft from down below. I heard the sound of Honey washing up. The clunk of the faucet when the water turned off. A short while later, Honey's voice rose up loud and clear to my loft.

"Eric." Her tone was firm. She cleared her voice. "I'd like to have a talk with you."

"Not now, Mom."

"Now," she said with iron in her voice. Then softer, "We have to talk, and there's no better time than the present. Let's go outside."

I heard the screen door to the porch slide open, followed by the sound of my dad's odd gait as he crossed the floor. Finally, I heard the door close. I waited, listening. I don't remember falling asleep.

CHAPTER 14

Today's a new day

"**J**AKE!"

Dad's voice shook me from my dreams. I blinked in the blinding light of the sun pouring in my window.

"Jake!" Dad hollered up the ladder.

Memories of the night before rushed back, and I grumbled as I put the pillow over my head. "What?" I screamed back.

"Get dressed, son. We've got to go."

"Go where?"

"Just get on down here," he commanded. "Please."

I tossed the pillow to the floor and stared at the ceiling. I had put glow-in-the-dark stars up there. At night they glowed this surreal green that felt magical. But in the daylight, they just looked like stupid pieces of plastic. Fake.

I dragged my feet as I climbed down the ladder and stepped into the living room, where my dad was standing, waiting for me. He was showered, shaved, and dressed in hiking shorts and a clean T-shirt. I could smell the scent of soap on his skin.

"What's going on?" I was confused. He hadn't showered in weeks. "Did you shave?"

He rubbed his cheek. "Yeah, the beard was starting to itch me. And"—he cleared his throat—"today's a new day."

I looked over his shoulder at Honey standing in the kitchen, listening. When she caught my eye, she moved her head to indicate I should pay attention to my father. Something was going on. Something felt different.

"So?" I said warily.

My dad took a breath, taking in my attitude. He clapped his hands together, and the sound startled me.

"So . . . ," he repeated. "I want to know if those kayaks you cleaned up are ready for us to take out on the water."

I felt his words wash over me, cleansing me of my anger and frustration, as I had washed the kayaks the day before. I felt all shiny inside, and full of hope. It must've shown on my face because Dad stepped closer, placed his hands on my shoulders, and leaned down to look me in the eyes.

"I'm sorry, son."

I was shocked to see tears in his eyes.

"Would you be willing to give your dad a do-over?"

I lunged forward and hugged him tight. He knew my answer without me saying it.

I'd be lying if I said it was easy getting the kayaks and paddles transported from Honey's house down to the kayak launch point in the golf carts. Chief Rand had the day off, so he joined us. Macon arrived wearing a wide-brimmed hat, a long-sleeved tan fishing shirt, thin cargo pants, and water shoes that outlined each toe.

"That's a nice look there, buddy!" Rand called out. "Like you just walked off the set of a nature safari show."

"Wow," Lovie said, walking up and giving him the full up and down eye treatment. "You're very . . . khaki."

Macon was unfazed by the teasing. "I'm protecting my skin." He pulled out a tube of sunscreen from one of his many pockets.

"Good thinking, Macon," Honey said, digging out a huge tube of sunscreen from her backpack to pass around to the others.

The launching point was an angled concrete slope along the creek's edge. It was designed so one person at a time could slide into his kayak, then push off into the shallow water.

"First, life jackets," Honey commanded. "Everybody put one on, and then I'll review the paddle maneuvers."

Macon's hands trembled as he tried to clip his life jacket's buckles. This was his first time in a kayak. His first time going into murky water. Up till now, he'd only swum in swimming pools. And even that was new for him.

"I can't believe I'm doing this," he muttered. My dad went to stand next to him and helped him buckle up.

"I admit I'm feeling the same way."

"But I've never done this before. *You* have."

Dad placed a hand on his shoulder and gave him a gentle shake. "We'll try. *Together*. Okay?"

Macon blew out a plume of air. "What happens if I fall out?"

"You'll get wet," Dad replied, smiling. "And you'll float. That's what these are for." He tugged at his life jacket.

"Yeah. Okay," said Macon.

Honey put us in groups of three. "That's called the buddy system," she told us. "In case someone needs help." Lovie and Macon were in her buddy pack. Dad and I paired up with Chief Rand.

Honey went over the basic strokes, giving Macon a chance to practice on dry land before getting into the water. His broad shoulders easily maneuvered the paddle. I think even he was surprised at how easy it was.

"Okay, then!" Honey called out. "Let's get wet!"

"You can do it," Lovie said to Macon.

I gave him two thumbs up.

Chief Rand and Dad talked quietly together, formulating their action plan, while I got my vest on and pulled my kayak to the water's edge.

"It'll be like riding a bike," I heard Rand say to my dad. "Once you get in that kayak, all your skills will come back to you."

"Muscle memory," said Dad.

Chief Rand grinned widely and gave a firm slap to my father's shoulder. "You ready?"

Dad gave a quick nod. Chief Rand pulled his kayak to the launch ramp next to mine. I held my breath. All eyes were on Dad. I glanced at Honey. Her lips were moving in prayer.

Kayaks were tippy when you got in. Rand stuck by his friend's side, holding the kayak steady as Dad slowly eased down into the cockpit. His brows were knitted tight, and I knew he was planning every movement he made in advance. He had no choice. I saw him plan out everything in his daily life. Or risk falling. Day after day, whether it was answering the door, going to the bathroom, getting a cup of water, or getting into a kayak. All of it took a lot of work. And courage. There had to be a special kind of fear about going into the water missing a limb. I was never prouder of my dad than I was at that moment.

Once in the cockpit, Dad used his muscled arms to get properly seated. Then, to my surprise, he handed his prosthetic to Chief Rand. Never had my dad done that in public.

He looked over at me. "Here goes nothing, son."

I gave him two thumbs up.

Chief Rand stood at the water's edge, ready to help in case there was trouble. We all watched my dad adjust his weight.

Next, he used his paddle to slowly push away from the land. He took a few gentle strokes with the paddle, testing out his forward motion. Then he tried paddling backward. Next, the turn strokes.

We all cheered when he was done.

"It's all about the balance," called out Honey.

Dad yelled out to Macon, "Your turn, big guy."

Lovie and Honey stayed close to Macon, coaching him every step of the way. Once he settled into the cockpit of his kayak, Macon's concentrated expression eased and he grinned, hoisting his paddle in victory.

"Hop in, Rand!" Honey called out from her kayak. "This train's leaving the station. Choo! Choo!"

Honey took the lead, her paddles dipping into the water with an easy rhythm. Chief Rand stayed in the back this time. "I'm the caboose of this kayak train," he called out. I think we all knew he was just saying that to keep an eye on my dad.

The colorful kayak convoy stretched out along the creek. We paddled against the slow current, each of us moving at our own speed. It wasn't a race. But all of us made sure we didn't lose sight of our buddy group.

Left stroke, right stroke. Left stroke, right stroke.

I started to feel some muscle burn trying to keep up with my dad. His arm muscles were strong, giving him a steady rhythm. Left to right, side to side, he glided across the still water, creating a gentle ripple behind him. No one could keep up with him. He could turn with ease, slide backward without a problem, alternating his paddle from side to side. In fact, he looked pretty darn good out there. I laughed, knowing he knew it too.

We reached a small cove where the cordgrass rose above us like a jungle. We took a moment to catch our breath and let our kayaks float lazily in the current. The marsh was alive with little pops and snaps. Even the grasses made their own soft noises. I watched my dad glide up to Macon and high-five him with the end of his paddle.

"Looking good. You'll be a pro at this in no time."

Macon looked pleased at how well he was doing. It was no surprise to me. It was only a year ago that he'd learned to swim. I remembered how fast he could cut through the water at swimming practice. After a lifetime of being afraid of the water, Macon was turning out to be a natural in water sports.

Lovie paddled up to Macon's side and gave him some pointers. I watched and remembered how kind she was when she'd taught me to kayak, too. There wasn't a girl who knew more about living in the Lowcountry than Lovie Legare.

Dad took the lead as we headed back to the launching site. He made kayaking look so easy. I had a sheen of sweat from the effort by the time I finally caught up to him. "Wait up!" I called out. I put my heart into my paddling, giving each stroke a strong thrust.

He turned and, seeing me pushing toward him, rested

his paddle across his kayak and waited. Little silver fish leaped out of the water around us from time to time, moving like skipping stones across the water's surface before disappearing below. When I neared, he reached out to pull my kayak closer.

"You're getting really good at this," he said.

"Yeah," I said, basking in his praise. "Lovie taught me how."

"Really?" Emotions flickered across his face. "I wasn't even aware." His expression shifted. "I'm really glad we did this," he said. "Together."

I felt my emotions rise. "Me too."

In the silence, I heard the water lap against the sides of our kayaks. Dad looked out over the vast acres of green Spartina, so I took the moment to study him. It was different seeing him in the kayak, his legs hidden by it. I didn't see him as injured. His muscles were strong and tanned, and out on the water he could paddle faster than anyone else. He was his old self. The confident dad I missed.

Dad turned his head, and when he looked at me, his eyes bored into me.

"I'm proud of you, son," he began. "It took courage to tell me the truth last night."

"I'm sorry I blew up."

"I needed to hear it," he said. Then his voice lowered. "I hope I never disappoint you again."

A single pelican glided by us, low. Its body coasted just a

few feet above the water's surface. Dad smiled and straightened his shoulders. "I feel like that pelican right now," he said. He laughed and grinned widely.

"Free as a bird! Come on!"

He picked up his paddle and began skimming swiftly across the water, every bit as graceful as that pelican.

CHAPTER 15

Sometimes you have to let go of the past to be free to live your future

"WHO'S READY TO FIND THAT TREE fort today?" Dad yelled out.

A week had passed, and each day Dad and I took the kayaks out together. Dad was really into it. He woke up early every morning, called me down, and had breakfast ready, which we wolfed down. Then off we went to the water before the sun got too high and hot in the sky.

"I am!" I said.

He gently tugged on the bill of my ball cap.

The Islanders gathered at the dock, and I was pumped to see that all three of us were wearing our new khaki ball caps with THE ISLANDERS emblazoned on the front. Lovie helped me carry my kayak to the water's edge.

"You dad's really getting into the treasure hunt now," she said.

"I wonder if he's more excited about the treasure or finding his old tree fort."

Once we got all the kayaks unloaded, Dad called us together.

"Let's go over the plan one more time, team." Dad laid out our map on the back seat of his golf cart. He traced his finger over the map, revealing our mission.

"Jake, Honey, and I will travel by kayak, paddling east to this curve, then go northwest to here," he said. "This is where we get out." He looked at Chief Rand. "Rand, Macon, Lovie, and Lucky will travel by cart to the trail. After which, you'll go on foot to"—he tapped the map—"here."

"You mean where the trees make the X in the sky?" Lovie asked.

"That's correct," he said, tapping the spot on the map that marked our first, failed attempt at finding the old tree fort. Then he slid his finger over. "And this is our rendezvous point. Lone Cedar Dock."

Rand nodded a confirmation.

"Roger that," Macon said.

Dad glanced at his watch. "We're approaching twelve hundred hours. If we get going, that puts the water team on site by"—he paused, making calculations in his head—"thirteen hundred hours."

Lovie furrowed her brows. "What does that even mean?"

"Military time," I said. "That's one p.m." I could feel my excitement growing. Having Rand and Dad along made this mission seem real, not just a game.

Dad continued. "Land team, you'll do reconnaissance on the trail while you're waiting on us."

I leaned closer to Lovie and said, "That's military for check out the area to see what's what and where."

"Rand," Dad said, "you've got the supplies for trail clearing, right?"

"Boots. Hatchet. Honey did a right fine job." He readjusted the supplies in his backpack.

"I've got my metal detector, sir!" Macon called out, getting into the whole military mission vibe.

"Well done, soldier," Dad said.

I was proud to see Dad like this. Outdoors again and on a mission. And treating us like his team. Watching him, I thought back to all the times he was deployed with the Army, and I'd be home wondering what his life was like when he was away. He was a great leader. And he had medals and rank to prove it.

Neither of my friends was looking at Dad's legs now. He was wearing gray fishing shorts, which showed his prosthesis. I liked that he wasn't trying to hide it.

"Once our teams meet at the rendezvous," Dad concluded, "we'll follow the final riddle clues to the tree." He straightened. "Is everyone clear about our mission, team?"

"Let's go find the tree to find the treasure!" I yelled.

"Yeah!" everyone shouted and clapped their hands.

Out on a saltwater creek is a different world. Gone was the stability of the Earth where I walked one foot in front of the other. Here I glided like an otter across the water, following the winding path between bright green cordgrass that loomed high above my head. The tide was low and the smell of the pluff mud filled the air. Some people thought it stunk like rotten eggs, but to those of us who live in the Lowcountry, it smelled like home.

There was no noise except for the high-pitched cries of the ospreys and the lapping sound my paddle made with each stroke. From higher in the sky, I heard the hum of a plane flying by.

"Keep up!" Dad called to me over his shoulder.

I stopped daydreaming and pulled on the paddle harder, catching my left-right, left-right rhythm. My back muscles strained—it was hard to catch up with Dad. He made it all look so easy. I glanced over my shoulder to check on Honey. She was lagging far behind.

"Come on, Honey!" I called back to her.

"You guys go on ahead!" she yelled out. "I'm slow and steady back here. I'll catch up."

"But the team is always supposed to stick together!"

"I'm good," Honey called. She waved her hand, indicating I should go on. I waved back, then continued to push hard. My dad had stopped and was waiting for me to catch up. I was panting hard when I pulled beside him.

"Good job," he said.

I looked behind us. Honey was nowhere in sight in the winding creek. "Where's Honey?"

"Don't worry about Honey. I can still see the top of her blue sun hat way back there. And"—he smiled at me—"you know she stops a dozen times to look at any creature that comes her way."

"True!" I laughed. "She even calls herself a nature nerd." I remembered the Invaders called us the same thing. Suddenly I felt proud to be called that.

Dad threw his head back, laughing. "We need to print that on a T-shirt for her."

Just then, a faint splash behind my kayak caught my attention. I jerked my head toward the sound.

"What is it?" Dad asked. "You see something?"

Scanning the water, I caught sight of movement in the water. Tracking it, I soon saw the telltale two eyes of an alligator rise up from below the surface.

"There!" I pointed, keeping my voice low, unsure of what I saw. My muscles tensed.

Dad rotated his head, slowly scanning the water with me. "I see it! At two o'clock." The military used the hands of a clock to give a visual location. If you are facing forward, straight ahead is twelve o'clock. Directly behind you is your six o'clock.

"What should we do?" My body was frozen.

"Stay calm," Dad said. "Alligators are usually afraid of

humans and keep their distance. We're in this fellow's home, don't forget. Our splashing around probably caught his attention. Let's wait and let him pass."

It was one thing to watch an alligator from the high safety of the dock. It was another to be in the water with it. I held my breath and sat motionless. The alligator steadily moved toward us, as sleek and smooth as a submarine, but Dad was right. When it got close, the alligator sank down into the water. I scanned the surface. It popped up again three feet off, heading for the bank.

"Let's go," Dad called out, and we took off again.

Suddenly, the calm, flat water began to ripple and churn. Before I could even say a word, gray fins broke the surface. Then a glistening gray body arched over the water before diving back in.

"Dolphins!" we both yelled.

Two dolphins swam near our kayaks, so close I could see their snouts as they popped up. Then they disappeared under the water. Dad and I stopped paddling and let the current drag us as we scanned the water, hope beating in our chests. What was it about these creatures that drew us to them? I just knew I wanted them to come back.

Suddenly, the two dolphins emerged again, this time only a few feet away. Then, to our delight, two more arched out of the water. Both Dad and I laughed out loud with surprise. We had four dolphins swimming around us, so close that I could hear the percussive *whoosh* of air pushed out of

"Nice work, man!" Rand said to my dad before they launched into some kind of secret handshake, laughing. I imagined them as kids, the same age as me when they played in these waters, best friends. I looked over at Macon and Lovie and hoped that we'd still be best friends when we were their age.

Macon handed us our hiking boots and Lovie passed out bug spray.

"Armor up, gentlemen!" Lovie commanded, holding out a can of bug spray in one hand and scratching her thigh with the other hand. "Or get devoured by those blood-sucking mosquitoes!"

"Where's Honey?" Macon asked, looking back along the creek.

I could see my grandmother approaching. "There she is." I waved my hands. "Honey, we're here!"

Honey waved back. "You go on," she called out.

Dad clapped his hands together. "Okay then. Let's take a look at that riddle."

"Yes, sir." I opened up my backpack and pulled out the blue leather journal. As my friends crowded around me, I flipped open to the marked page. "Okay, everyone, here's the next clue." I read aloud.

Turn straight to the northern tide.
Then walk west because the tree must hide.

"Which way is west right now?" Lovie asked. "We don't have a compass."

"That's easy," Macon said. He looked up at the sky and swung his arm toward the sun. "We know the sun rises in the east over our beach." He pointed through the trees. "Which is that way. And since the sun always sets in the west"—he step-turned and pointed in the opposite direction—"west is . . . there."

Dad looked up from the island map he was studying. "Good job, Macon. You're right on."

"But that's where we just came from," said Lovie. "We have to go back?"

"No," I replied. "We need to be looking from the tree line."

"Oh, I get it," Lovie said, nodding. "We have to start where the trees make the X."

Chief Rand nodded. "That's right. We have to go back to where X marked the spot. Be careful now. I'll make the path, but watch where you step. There are snakes."

We all looked warily around our feet.

"At least the ground is dry," said Dad.

"Yeah, we won't lose our new boots in the mud."

Lovie caught my eye and laughed.

We all got into a line and began our trek into the maritime forest to head toward where X marked the spot in our last clue.

Chief Rand led the way, weaving through the morass of vines and shrubs, creating a trail.

"I feel like a real explorer doing this," Lovie said, pushing aside a spiderweb. "I wonder if pirates did this."

"I'd imagine so," my dad replied. He carefully ducked beneath some low-hanging limbs. "And not just pirates. The Native Americans too. People have found bits of their clay pottery all around these parts. And other artifacts like marbles, glass bottles, and tools."

"Don't forget the cannonball I found as a kid!" Chief Rand yelled out from the front of the line.

"*We* found," Dad called back. "The museum said that it was from the Revolutionary War period."

Chief Rand lifted his hand to indicate we should halt. He was staring up. After a minute he turned his head, a grin slowly stretching across his face. "You know," he said with wonder, "I think this is it."

We all clustered around him and followed to where he pointed. The dense forest had cleared out to a field of wild grasses and a few palmettos. A single tree stood in the center. It was much bigger and wider than the others, with broad, muscled limbs that stretched far out over the marsh. It looked ancient, a grandfather of the forest. A mighty live oak.

Dad crossed his arms and tilted his head in thought. "Are you sure? It looks different from what I remember."

"Of course it does. That was more than thirty years ago," replied Chief Rand.

I checked the riddle and read aloud.

It's disguised as a huge beast
With big ogre feet and arms that stretch east.

"Well, it sure looks like a beast," Dad said with amusement.

"What are we waiting for?" asked Lovie, and she took off for the tree.

"Check out the base of this tree," I shouted, running after her.

"There she goes again," cried Macon as he followed us.

When I reached the massive tree, I wandered around it slowly. The roots emerged from the ground all thick, knotted, and gnarled. "Ogre feet!" I cried with excitement. I stretched my arms out against the trunk. "Look how big it is."

"This tree is huge," cried Lovie. "I'd build a fort here for sure."

Chief Rand and Dad strode up beside us. I could see they were as excited as us kids. Dad walked up to the tree and rested his hand against the thick gray ridges of the massive trunk.

"Hello, old friend."

Macon looked troubled. "Something doesn't add up. The riddle says *arms that stretch east*. I'm guessing arms are the branches, right?" When we agreed, he continued. "But east is this way." He pointed back toward the way we just walked. "Look. There's nothing here. No arm."

Dad's brows knitted. "I'm pretty sure this is the tree. But I see your point. Let me read the rest of the riddle."

Around her waist is a rope.
Use it to climb with strength and with hope.

Don't fear you're not strong enough.
Use the steps to climb all the way up.

Find where a wise owl might be.
There you'll find the treasure from the sea.

Find where a wise owl might be.
That's where it's hidden,
The treasure from the sea.

Macon craned his neck and looked up as he walked around the base of the tree. "I don't see any rope."

Lovie and I followed Macon around the tree, and we didn't see any rope either.

"Jake," Dad called, "what's under all this old debris?" He used his boot to sweep away a thick layer of rotting oak leaves.

Macon tossed me a small hand shovel, and I slowly started to pull back the layers at the base of the tree. Each layer was darker and wetter the deeper I dug.

Lovie hopped up on a small log and walked on it like a balance beam.

"Careful there," Rand said. "That log looks weak and . . ." His voice trailed off as he looked from the log up to the tree. "Check out the tree scar."

We all looked up to where he was pointing.

"That section looks like it split off from the rest of the tree a long time ago," Rand said. "See how it's jagged and black? Sometimes a large limb will fall away from the sheer weight. Or it could've been some weakness in the wood."

"Poor tree," Lovie crooned.

Chief Rand turned to point at the log Lovie was still standing on, then laughed. "I reckon that right there is the remnant of the branch."

Dad called out, "That's the branch that bent down low! We threw a rope over it to hoist ourselves up to climb."

Chief Rand rubbed his beard. "Yup, I remember now, too. This is where you broke your arm that summer."

In a flash I remembered the photograph I'd found in the loft. My dad and Rand, or Red as my dad called him back when they were boys, were hanging from a tree limb.

"Well, dang," Macon said, finally satisfied. "Then this here is the old tree. Now where's the fort?"

"We have a Doubting Thomas on the team," Chief Rand said with amusement.

"He just likes to be sure of his facts," said Lovie in Macon's defense.

"Good man," said Dad.

My shovel hit something in the soil. "Hey, y'all! I found something."

Everyone drew close as I unearthed a bit of rope from the compost. It was the color of dirt and mold, and it was falling apart as I lifted it.

"That's the rope!" Dad exclaimed. He was as excited now as us kids.

Lovie, Macon, and I hooted out loud at this proof.

Macon was holding on to his cap with one hand and looking far up the tree. "So where's the fort?"

We all craned our necks to peer up at the massive tree. Up high, the branches were crisscrossed and clusters of leaves camouflaged anything that might be lurking among them.

"There!" Lovie called out. She was using her binoculars. "I see wood up there. It looks like it could be part of the floor of a tree fort." She handed the binoculars to my dad.

As he looked up, his grin stretched across his face. "Yep, that's it," he said. He turned to Rand. "Hey, pal. We found it!"

Rand came closer to slap my dad on the back. "Yes, we did." They shook hands, laughing. I hadn't seen my dad laugh and smile so much in a long time. I could almost see the years fall away and they were kids again, like us Islanders.

"How can we get up there?" I asked, eager to start climbing.

"The fort's in pieces, buddy," Dad said.

"But we have to find the treasure," I said urgently.

"We can get up there!" Macon exclaimed. Now that he was convinced we'd found the tree fort, he was primed and ready to find the treasure.

"Oh no you can't," Dad said firmly with a shake of his head.

"But we came all this way. We've got to. We can't give up," I argued.

He let out a deep breath. "It's not giving up. We have to remember how old this fort is. Look at what happened to the limb. The tree fort is falling apart. There's hardly anything left of it. It's not safe. Plus, if anything was up there, it's not now. It's just a bunch of loose boards. I'm sorry, Jake. We have to figure out a new plan."

All the excitement I'd felt crumbled like the dry, brittle twigs under my boot. I couldn't just walk away from this. Just as I was about ready to argue with him, a voice broke through the forest.

"Yoo-hoo! I've got lunch!" Honey pushed through a section of brush and young palmetto fronds, smiling from ear to ear. She stopped and looked skyward. "Well, I'll be. You found it!" she exclaimed. And then tripped.

"Mom!" Dad and Rand hurried to her side to take her arm.

"I'm fine," she said, brushing them away. "Dang tree roots."

Honey set down her backpack. It landed with a thud. "I packed a good lunch. What do you say we take a break?"

I looked down at where it landed, and something poked out from the ground covering. I walked over to take a closer look. I squatted down and, using the shovel, dug into the earth. Under a layer of soil, I saw something faded orange and white. I dug my fingers below the edges and eased it out of the ground.

"What's this thing?" I asked as I lifted a mud-encrusted plastic cylinder by the handle.

"No way!" Chief Rand took it from my hands and walked closer to Dad. He wiped the dirt from the canister. "This is my old camping thermos! Man, I took this with me everywhere. I was crushed when I lost this." He rolled it in his hands. "And look, my name's still on it!" He pointed at his name etched into the side.

"Dad, that thermos is a sign. The treasure has got to be here. We have to find it."

"Well, you can't solve a problem on an empty stomach," Honey interrupted, tossing a peanut butter and jelly sandwich at me.

She was right. I was starving after all the paddling and hiking. We gathered in a circle to sit on the dirt and ate PB&Js, apples, and granola bars and drank water from our thermoses.

Macon was the first to finish his lunch. He grabbed his metal detector, which he had lugged all the way through the forest. "I was thinking," he said. "Chief Rand's thermos was probably in the old tree fort. So if that fell down, maybe some other things did too."

"The metal box," I said, and sprang to my feet.

Macon put on the metal detector headset and started walking slowly around the base of the tree, waving the machine in the same back and forth movement he'd used on the beach.

Lovie came to my side, carrying the journal. "It says the treasure is hidden *where a wise owl might be.*" Lovie shielded her eyes as she looked up the trunk. "Owls live in holes in a tree. So that means it's hiding somewhere up there."

"That's not the problem." I stuffed my lunch trash in the side pocket of my backpack. "Getting *up* there is."

I pointed to a few old boards nailed to the tree's trunk. "Look. Those have to be the steps in the riddle, right?"

"They are. Good eye. But even if you could reach them," Dad said, "those boards are rotten. I can't imagine the number of storms and hurricanes they've weathered. It's just gone, kids." He paused, then said with meaning, "Sometimes we have to accept when there's nothing left." He sighed. "Sometimes you have to let go of the past to be free to live your future."

I knew he was talking about his leg—and so much more. I caught a glimpse of what it must've felt like to be told to let go of his leg. How hard it was. Because I didn't want to let go of finding our treasure. Not yet.

"Guys!" Macon yelled.

"What?" Lovie and I spun around.

"My metal detector is picking up something." He waved it over a small area. "Right here!" He held his detector in place.

Chief Rand hurried over with the hatchet and cut away some tangled vines. When he was done, I dropped to my knees and used the shovel to dig. Everyone formed a circle around me as I pulled back a thick layer of decaying leaves.

Clunk.

The shovel hit something metal. Something was down in there. I paused and met my father's gaze. I saw hope kindling there. Feeling excitement flood my veins, I dropped the shovel and dug with my bare fingers into the moist, cool earth, which was more compost than soil. A fat earthworm slithered away, but I kept digging down until I could free the hard edges of a metal box. Slowly, carefully, I lifted the box from its grave.

Lovie reached out to gently swipe away the soil from the top, revealing a cracked wooden handle. Dad and Chief Rand sucked in their breath at the sight.

"I can't believe it," Dad said in a low voice.

"I'm stunned," said Rand.

"Is this the treasure box?" Lovie asked.

"Sure is," Dad said, and reached out to take the box from my hands.

We kids began hooting and jumping up and down, giving each other high-fives, shouting, "We found it!" and, "Good job, Macon!"

"You guys!" cried Lovie. "This is a big moment! We have to take a picture."

We gathered in front of the great tree, arms around one another's shoulders, feeling like explorers and pirates at the same time. I held the box proudly in my arms. Nobody had to tell us to smile. We were all grinning widely.

"I don't remember much from childhood, but I do remember shoving the box in an old tree hole," said Dad.

"Right," piped in Lovie. "The wise old owl's tree hole."

"It's obvious that the tree limb fell, for whatever reason, and this box, and my thermos, fell right down with it," Rand said.

Honey added, "Life gives you unexpected surprises. Accept the gifts as they come with gratitude." She clapped her hands together. "Now quit yapping and open that thing up!"

I tried to open the box, then moaned with disappointment.

"What's wrong?" Lovie asked.

"It's locked." I was so frustrated I wanted to hurl the rusty, dirt-covered box to the ground to see if it would break open. I felt Dad's hand on my shoulder. I looked up and he offered me a smile.

"I know where that key is."

CHAPTER 16

One man's trash is another man's treasure

S TANDING AT THE BOTTOM OF THE LOFT
stairs, Dad called up to me. He couldn't climb up, so we
worked together to find the missing key.

"The key is hidden in one of the books in the bookcase."

I looked at the books and groaned. This was going to take forever. "There are over a hundred books up here."

"Book by book, son. It's in there. You'll find it."

"I'll try."

"Read the book titles. Think—where would *you* have hidden the key?"

"Okay," I called back.

I scratched my head, then walked to the wooden bookshelf that took up the wall. Determined, I started at the highest shelf and ran my finger across the spine of each book, one after the other, reading the titles. A lot of books were about animals, birds, shells, South Carolina history. I stopped at *Pirates and Privateers of the Americas*. Pirates had treasure chests, I thought. I pulled the thick book off the shelf and opened it. No key.

"Was it a pirate book?" I hollered.

"No, it has nothing to do with pirates. Find a title that has the word 'key' in it."

"Key. Okay."

I looked at three more shelves.

"No ... nope ... not that one ..."

A section of several blue-spined books made me pause. The Hardy Boys series. I scanned one title after the other: *The Three Investigators, Hunting for Hidden Gold, The Tower Treasure*. That one gave me pause. But the word 'key' wasn't in any of those titles. Then I stopped. The next title was *The Witchmaster's Key*.

My hand trembled as I slid the hardcover book from the shelf. As I did, something fell out from the worn, thin pages. I looked at the floor, and there lying by my shoes was a small key. My heart raced.

"Got it!" I shouted, and lifted the key high into the air.

The Islanders, Chief Rand, Honey, and Dad cheered from the bottom of the loft ladder when I climbed down. I reached out my arm and offered Dad the key. He shook his head.

"You do the honors, son. This was your idea. Your search for treasure."

My friends eagerly nodded their approval. Even Lucky barked.

We walked out to the porch, where the metal box sat on the coffee table. It was badly rusted. A few small holes had rusted clear through. It was also dented, creating jagged edges.

"Careful not to scratch yourself," Honey warned.

"Those dents are probably from it falling out of the tree," Macon said.

"It's been out in the woods for a long time," said Lovie.

I wiped away the grime from the keyhole and slid the key in it. It fit. I looked up at my friends and smiled. It didn't turn easily because of all the rust. I held my breath.

"Give it a good whap," Macon suggested.

"No, no," Honey cried, hands out. "It's fragile. Take your time."

After a little wiggling and gentle jiggling, I heard a faint *click*.

Everyone leaned in closer. The lid was bent and didn't open.

"Let me try," Dad said, and moved to sit in front of the box. He reached into his pocket and pulled out his Swiss Army knife. The blade eased around the edges of the box, scraping away rust and caked-on dirt. Then, after closing the knife, Dad put his long fingers around the edges of the box and gently jiggled the lid. The hinges creaked, but slowly, the lid eased open.

We all sucked in our breath.

"Before we look inside," Dad said, "just remember, this has been buried for more than twenty-five years. I have no memory of what I stuffed inside. I just really hope it's nothing embarrassing."

"Yeah, yeah, yeah," Rand teased. "Scared they'll see your old love letters from girlfriends or something?"

Dad snorted and we all laughed.

"I just hope there are no spiders," Lovie said.

"As long as the treasure map is in there," I said.

"Just open it!" exclaimed Honey. "I want to live long enough to see what's inside."

"Right," Dad said. "Here we go."

He pried open the lid. At the light, several little bugs scattered around in the dirt and crumbling leaves inside.

Macon sprang away from the box. "No bugs better jump out at me."

Lovie pinched her nose. "What's that smell?"

"It's just good old-fashioned decomposition," Honey replied. "Looks like water and dirt seeped in over time. That's just nature doing her thing."

Honey laid out a towel on the table. "But I don't want you getting any of that muck on my porch furniture. Here, use this, please."

Dad wiped his palms on his pants and began raking away the leaves and dirt. He pulled out the contents one by one.

First came a huge black shark's tooth that was almost the size of my palm.

"A megalodon tooth!" Macon exclaimed.

Honey reached down to pick up the tooth. "Well, sir, the

megalodon was the largest shark on the face of the Earth. And it's true people have found these ancient fossils right here in South Carolina. That's because this area used to be a seafloor. You'll find all kinds of shark fossils. Including this very large white shark's tooth. Not a megalodon tooth. Sorry. Though it's a big one!" She admired it a moment, then set it back on the towel.

Next Dad pulled out a mud-encrusted, wooden-handled pocketknife.

"I remember this one," Dad said fondly.

"You carried it everywhere," said Honey.

"It's seen better days." Dad laid it down on the towel. Next he pulled out a green canvas pouch, moldy and discolored. From inside, Dad pulled out a green plastic case and flipped it open on the hinge.

"Hey, I remember that," Rand exclaimed. "Our compass!"

"Yep." Dad set it on the towel. He gingerly moved around the mud as he scrounged around inside. "Got something." Slowly, he pulled out a metal chain loop with silver dog tags hanging from it.

"Oh, my!" Honey exclaimed, and brought her fingers to her mouth.

Dad met his mother's eyes. "These are Granddad's," he said. "Remember when he gave them to me?"

"On your twelfth birthday," Honey replied. Tears pooled as the memory played in her mind. "He said you were a man. It meant a lot for him to give those to you."

"I remember." He looked at the box. "That's it."

"What about the treasure map?" Disappointment was rising back up inside me.

"That's it, my boy."

"Some treasure," I said flatly. "Looks like a bunch of old junk."

"Now, son," Dad said admonishingly, "you know what they say. One man's trash is another man's treasure. Each of these things meant a whole lot to me at one time."

"Sorry," I said, but I didn't mean it.

"Hey, I get that you think it's junk," he said. "And you're disappointed. All of you. So am I. I could've sworn we had a treasure map in here." He looked back at Chief Rand for confirmation. Rand nodded in agreement.

I just couldn't give up. I bent over the box and poked my finger in the mud. It was sickeningly gooey, but I kept scraping away. I pulled out a piece of rolled-up paper, so wet and muddy it started falling apart in my hands. "Hey, what's this?"

Afraid I would tear it, I gently lifted it up between two fingers and laid it on the towel. A bit of frayed blue yarn tied around it was all that was keeping it together. It came off easily. I slowly unrolled the paper. It had turned the color of coffee over time.

Once upon a time, someone had drawn on the paper. Now, however, the ink marks were barely visible.

Lovie lowered her head to inspect closely. "There, see it? That looks like a big X."

I bent low to inspect. "Yeah! With a circle around it." I looked up at Dad, grinning. "It's the treasure map!"

The corners of Macon's mouth pulled downward. "Yeah, but look at it. What good is it? We can't read it."

"Yeah," I agreed, feeling my enthusiasm wither in my chest. I thought of all the time we'd spent planning the trip, all the effort getting through the maritime forest, all the mosquito bites! And yet all we found was a washed-out piece of paper we couldn't read. Time had erased the telling details.

"What a waste of time!" I grumbled, discouraged.

Dad placed a hand on my back. "I am sorry," he said. "I know you're disappointed. But remember, our mission was a success." He paused to look at each of us. "We set out to find the tree fort and we did. We also found the treasure map. That's a lot. Explorers have to take what they find and celebrate. I'm proud of you all."

I knew Dad was trying to cheer us up, but it wasn't working.

Dad put the lid back on the box and picked it up. He was turning it over in his hands to look at the bottom when there was a dull thud from inside.

"Did you hear that?" I asked, reaching toward the box. "Can I hold it again?"

Dad handed it over, looking as curious as I did.

Hope rose high in our hearts as I set the box back on the table. I paused, then put my hands on the lid.

"Careful," Lovie urged.

I pried open the lid again. The mud on the bottom had

shifted. I grimaced as I ran my fingers across the bottom of the box through the layer of muck, trying not to think about rolled-up centipedes. On the bottom of the box, I felt something mushy, like a piece of fabric. It was so thick with grime no one had noticed it wasn't the metal bottom. Scraping away mud, I caught a glimpse of blue. It was so stuck it seemed glued. My blood raced as I picked at the edge with the precision of a surgeon.

"What is it?" asked Macon.

"Something soft, like fabric. It's stuck pretty good to the bottom."

"Keep going," said Lovie.

Finally, I got a piece of the blue fabric between two fingers. Exhaling, I gently peeled it, bit by bit, from the bottom. I lifted it from the mud. As I let it hang from my fingers, we could see it was a blue pouch with a faded gold drawstring.

There was a collective gasp in the room.

Dad was sitting beside me on the wicker settee. He held open his hand for the pouch. Once it was in his palm, he felt the weight of the bag. "There's something in here." Excitement spread across his face.

Once more my heart rate zoomed. "Open it, Dad!"

Dad carefully pried open the mud-encrusted bag, then turned it upside down over the towel. Out tumbled three coins.

We cheered out loud. Macon did a victory dance.

"I'll be darned. It's our treasure!" Chief Rand exclaimed. He lifted one of the coins from the table and studied it with an expression of wonder. "I thought we'd lost these."

"I forgot about them," Dad said with a short laugh, taking hold of one and wiping mud from the surface. Then he flipped it over in his palm.

"Shiver me timbers! Ye found booty!" Macon declared. "Doubloons!"

"Only they're not gold," said Lovie in a soft voice.

"Nope. Never said they were," said Chief Rand.

I turned to Dad. "But your old journal said you buried it somewhere."

"I don't know. Guess I had a change of heart." He shook his head and handed me a coin. "Thank goodness that old tree held on to our secrets. Right?"

"Right!" I exclaimed, looking at the coin in my hand.

"You really did find a treasure," Macon said with awe.

"And we found it again!" I turned to my friends, feeling my chest expand. I put my arms around them, as they did around me. "We did it! We found a treasure!"

"We don't know what kind of coins they are though." Macon picked up a coin, taking his turn to look. "There's Spanish writing."

"They're old, that's for sure," I said. "They have to be valuable." I turned to Dad. "Right?"

"I honestly don't know," he replied. "We found them on the beach. I expect they washed ashore, and we came by at the right time."

"There might be more. Maybe a treasure chest."

Dad laughed. "Or not. We were excited just to find these three."

"You never checked them out?" Macon asked with a hint of disbelief.

Dad turned to Rand, and they both smiled sheepishly. "We always meant to."

"All right, crew!" Honey exclaimed. "Now let's discuss what to do with all this booty. A good pirate would split the treasure with his crew. You okay with that?" she asked Dad.

Dad and Chief Rand looked at each other, then shrugged.

"Seems fair to me," Dad said. "We all found it together."

"But, Dad, Blackbeard didn't want to share his treasure. He left some pirates stranded on the beach, sank a ship, and killed some others."

"Let's just say he wasn't very good at sharing," said Honey.

"There are no Blackbeards in this group," Dad said. "We share the bounty. Jake, since you're the one who started this adventure, you get first pick."

"But, Dad," I said, feeling like we were raiding his personal things. "Technically, this is all your stuff."

He ruffled my hair. "All right then. How 'bout I hold on to these coins?"

When we all protested, he laughed. "For the time being. Until we figure out their worth." He looked at the group. "So, what do you want?"

"Can I have the shark's tooth?" Lovie asked. "I collect them, and I have a lot, but I've never found one this big."

"Sure thing," my dad said. "I can't think of a better person to have it. Our naturalist." He lifted a brow and added, "You know, I found that way up at the northern tip of the island. After a hurricane skirted by us."

Lovie picked up the tooth and admired it in her hand. "I know where I'll be heading after the next big storm."

Honey reached over my shoulder and picked up the dog tags. "These belonged to my father." She ran her thumb across the information stamped onto the metal tags. "It'd mean a lot to me to have them back."

"Of course, Mom."

She held the dog tags close to her chest and headed into the house.

"Okay, now it's down to the compass and the pocketknife," he said.

"Chief Rand, you need a treasure," I said.

He held up the thermos we found in the forest. "I got my treasure already."

I looked over at my friend. "Macon, you pick."

"Nah, I don't feel right. These are your family things. *You* pick."

Dad picked up the remaining items and said, "How about I decide for the both of you?" He handed Macon the compass. "You are the one who located the box. I think it's fitting that you have the compass. It's an old military-issued one that also belonged to my granddad."

"That's really cool, Mr. Potter." He smiled. "Thanks."

Dad said to me, "I like the idea of giving you my favorite pocketknife." He pulled one of the blades out of the smooth wooden handle. "It just needs a little cleaning and sharpening, and then this knife will last you a lifetime." He flipped the blade back down into the handle, then handed it to me. "This little thing went with me everywhere I went on this island. It's helped me out many times in the woods. Like you've helped me, son."

"Thanks, Dad." I took the knife and inspected it. It was right up there with my journal for my favorite things. "I guess all that's left to do is figure out what kind of coins you have, Dad. What if they're worth a ton of money? We could be rich!"

He laughed. "Hold on, now. Maybe not rich. But I'd say they have some value. I just don't know who to talk to about these kinds of things."

Honey walked back onto the porch, setting down a tray with cups and a pitcher of lemonade. "There's one person who just happens to live on this island who knows a lot about treasures. I'll bet he'll know exactly what those coins are."

Lovie and Macon shot looks at me, and my stomach hit my feet. We all knew who Honey was talking about.

Scary Harry!

huge black
shark tooth

Compass

dog
tags

treasure map

muddy
pocketknife

old
coins

CHAPTER 17

Real friendship was about loving each other enough to be honest

I T TOOK US TWO DAYS JUST TO BUILD UP THE courage to go, but I regretted the plan the moment we saw the sign: HAROLD MAYNARD, DEWEES ISLAND, SC.

The property came with an additional warning. Stapled to a tree trunk was a red plastic sign, cloaked in Halloween-like spider webs, that read: NO TRESPASSING. PRIVATE PROPERTY.

I stomped on the brake of the golf cart. Macon and Lovie lurched forward.

"What the heck?" asked Macon.

"I don't think that sign's even allowed," Lovie whispered.

We stared at the scene in grim silence. The house looked

really unkempt, like no one cared. Vines dangled from the thick cloak of trees.

"I know we're supposed to keep things natural on the island, but this is going too far," I said.

Macon slapped another mosquito on his arm. "Light can't get through that mess, but mosquitoes do just fine."

"I can't do this, guys." Lovie chewed on the corner of her lower lip. "It looks too creepy in there."

Macon leaned in from the back seat, his head between Lovie's and mine. "Not to mention, he's got all those scars on his hands and his neck."

Lovie's eyes got big. "How do you think he got them?"

"Who knows? Maybe he's got a bad secret that sent him to prison," Macon said, warming to the topic. "But he escaped and is hiding out here."

I poked Macon in the side as Lovie's face paled at the word "prison."

"I'm sorry," Macon blurted, catching on. "I . . . I didn't mean . . ."

"It's okay," Lovie said quietly, looking down at her hands.

The fact that her biological dad was in prison was her biggest secret. Lovie was gripping her necklace turtle charm, sliding it back and forth in little rapid movements.

"Doofus, lay off the dramatics. Honey told me he got the scars in the Vietnam War. He's actually some kind of war hero."

"Oh, wow," Macon said, and slid back on his seat. "Now I really feel like a jerk."

"It's okay. Really . . . ," Lovie said.

I thought now was as good a time as any to ask Lovie about the letter she mailed him last summer. "Hey, uh, so you said you heard back from your dad?"

Macon poked me from the back seat.

Lovie looked away. "Yes," she answered quietly. "The letter arrived back in the spring." She shrugged. "Mom got mad at me for going behind her back. But still, it was nice to hear from him. He told me how much my letter meant to him." A quick smile spread across her face, then just as quickly, disappeared. She looked at me, then at Macon in the back seat. "This is an Islanders secret, okay?"

Macon and I nodded.

"I wrote him back. My mom will be so upset if she finds out. But what choice did she give me? She gets mad if I go behind her back, but she forbids me to write to him. I mean, he's my dad, right? So please, promise you won't tell anyone."

"I promise," I said.

Macon shrugged. "Who am I going to tell?"

Lovie glared at him.

Macon made the gesture of locking his lips closed and throwing away the key.

Lovie faced the road again. "I don't want to talk about it anymore." She sat straighter and looked out at the house. "I can't even see Scary Harry's house," she said, changing the subject.

I wanted to ask what his letter said, but I let it go. For now.

"Isn't it weird that his house is so far away from everyone else's?" I asked.

"Yeah," Macon said. "It's at the edge of the forest, way out on the island's tip. I'm guessing the guy's not very social."

"He isn't," said Lovie. "I overheard Aunt Sissy tell a neighbor once that the man never leaves his house except to walk the beach."

"Never?" Macon asked.

"Nope. Never," Lovie replied. "He doesn't hang out with anyone. Doesn't go to any island events or meetings. Or even ride the ferry."

"What does he eat?"

Macon made a grisly face. "Maybe those spiders? Or your favorite . . . raccoons."

"Gross," I said.

Macon's expression shifted, and he whispered, "Are we doing this or not?"

I flexed my fingers on the steering wheel, trying to build up the courage to turn onto the path toward Scary Harry's house.

"You're the one who wants to know what the treasure is," Macon reminded me. I swallowed down my nerves and turned very slowly onto the overgrown pathway.

"What's the worst that could happen? I mean, he's just an old man," I said, trying to convince myself.

I pressed the pedal and began creeping forward along the rutted dirt path. The tree branches arched over us like the ribs inside a beast. I gripped the wheel tightly. Suddenly, several gray mourning doves started up from the brush in a squawking panic.

"Aaaah!" we all shrieked.

I swung the cart around and sped back to the main road.

"That was terrifying!" Lovie was the first person to speak.

"Whatever. I would have gone up to Scary Harry"—Macon turned toward me—"but you zoomed off like a big ol' chicken before we could even see the man's house."

"Yeah, right! You were scared. I saw your face."

He shook his head in denial.

"Okay then. I'll turn around right now and drop you off at his driveway." I slowed the cart to a stop and cranked the steering wheel, pretending to turn around. "Then you can go ask him about the coins *yourself*."

Macon's eyes widened. "No way I'm going in there alone."

"Bawk bawk bawk," I teased him.

"Whatever." Macon put his hands up to look like claws and made a hissing sound like the raccoon.

I pressed my lips together, trying not to laugh.

"If you boys are done fooling around, how about we scope out his house from the water?" asked Lovie.

"How would we do that?" I asked.

"We go for a boat ride, of course."

"If you're asking me to go on the boat, no thanks." Macon still wasn't a big fan of open water.

We turned to him with our palms pressed together. "Come on. Pleeeease. We'll wear life jackets."

Macon let out a loud sigh. "Only on one condition."

"Name it," Lovie replied.

"You won't go fast. Promise?"

Lovie looked up in the air. We all knew Lovie liked to go fast.

She stuck out her hand. "Deal."

There were three important rules to remember before going out on a boat:

Check the weather before you go.

Have enough life jackets on board for everyone.

Leave a float plan with someone you trust.

At the dock, Lovie checked her boat for life jackets. We were all good there.

Then we raced up to the Nature Center to tell Honey our boating plans. Macon wanted to check the hourly weather conditions. Just as we reached the top of the stairs, we ran into Eddie and Andy, hovering over the touch tank on the porch.

Once again, in typical fashion, they were doing something obnoxious.

"Lookie what I caught!" Eddie was clutching a small fish in his hands. He held it up in Lovie's face.

"Hey, fish brains," Lovie said, unimpressed. "Put that flounder back in there. It's called a touch tank. Not a take-it-out tank."

"Is it a fish? Really?" Andy said in a drawl. "I mean, if a fish could be a pancake, then that's what a flounder is."

With its round, flat body and its two eyes on one side of its body, it was definitely a funny-looking fish. A short laugh slipped out of me.

"What are you laughing at?" Eddie asked menacingly.

"You look like a dork standing there holding a flounder," I said, not backing down.

"Cut it out, you guys," Lovie said sharply. She turned to Eddie. "You'd better put that fish back in the tank before Honey catches you."

Eddie shrugged, but he put the fish back in the tank. It landed with a soft splash.

"We were just having some fun," Andy defended his cousin.

"Whatever," Lovie said. She was about to turn away, but she paused and said to Eddie and Andy, "You know, it's sad. You guys have no idea of how to have fun." With that, she lifted her chin and walked into the Nature Center.

We followed after her, grinning ear to ear. Lovie had just served notice to the Invaders.

Back at the dock, Lovie leaped with ease onto her boat. It was a small, all-purpose fishing boat that served to transport her to Dewees Island from Isle of Palms. I loved that boat. It was fire-engine red with a center console. Lovie was proud of her ride and kept it clean and shiny. I openly admitted I was jealous not only of her boat, but of Lovie's knowledge of boating. She was happiest on the water and moved with the grace and speed of a seasoned sailor.

"It's time to set sail, me buccaneers!" she called out, tossing each of us a life jacket. "Jake, get the lines."

"Aye, aye, captain!" I was proud I knew how to unwind the

rope from the metal cleat on the dock. "All set, captain!" I leaped back on the boat.

"Hey, landlubber . . ." She pointed at Macon from the helm of the boat. "You good?"

"Yo ho," he said sarcastically, and twirled a finger in the air.

Lovie stood wide-legged in front of the console and fired up her single engine. It sprang to action, gurgling loudly as it churned the water. Time for joking was over as she carefully maneuvered the boat away from the dock. Macon and I sat on the small bench in front while she eased the boat to the middle of the channel. Then Lovie swung her head around and yelled, "Who's ready to see how fast this baby goes?"

Macon's face dropped.

Lovie burst out laughing. "Why didn't I get that on video?"

Macon smirked. "Don't mess with me, scallywag, or I'll split you in two."

I laughed, knowing he was just masking his relief.

We cruised at an easy speed around Dewees Island. The sun was still high in the sky, poking out between rolling clouds. Pelicans perched on top of big, bobbing cylindrical buoys with cone-shaped tops.

"What are those things?" Macon asked.

"They're channel markers," replied Lovie. "They help boaters navigate through the waterway. Forks in the channel, sand bars, things like that."

I could see Macon's reflection in her polarized lenses when she glanced at us.

"But why are they different shapes and colors?" Macon asked. When he wasn't full of facts, he was full of questions.

"Jake, you tell him."

I hoped I remembered it all correctly. It had been a whole year since I studied all this stuff to earn my boater education card.

"*Red and green, stay in between.* Right, Lovie?"

"Yep. What about the shapes and numbers?"

"The squares are always green. If they're on your right side, you're heading out toward the ocean, like we are now." I leaned my hand over the left side of the boat to feel the cool water flow by. "Triangles are always red. You keep them on your right side—the starboard side—to help you get back to your home port."

"Good job, matey!" Lovie said.

"And the numbers tell you how far you are from the ocean," I added.

"Okay, that's really cool to know," Macon said, nodding with appreciation. I could almost hear his brain clicking. "Next time I ride the ferry, I'll study the markers."

Three Jet Skiers blew past us, high rooster tails of water shooting out behind them.

"Hey, I recognize this stretch of beach," Macon said, shifting on his bench seat. "Look, there's the gazebo!"

We all looked over at what we called our beach headquarters. It looked so small from here.

"Hey, Lovie, do you have binoculars on the boat?" Macon asked.

"Of course. Why?" She reached into her console compartment for them.

"Hand them over. I see something moving in the dead trees." He stretched his arm out to grab them.

Lovie pulled back on the motor to slow down. We bobbed like a buoy as Macon focused his binoculars.

"Oh, this is epic. A coyote!" Macon handed me the binoculars.

I spied a lone coyote romping on the beach, tossing a ghost crab. I had to laugh. "It's like he's playing with his food."

"I want to see too," Lovie said, reaching out for the binoculars. After a few minutes she returned them to Macon. "It's crazy to see how they camouflage with the shoreline," she said. "How did you even spot this, Macon?"

He shrugged. "I've got a good eye, I guess."

"See?" she said with a smug smile. "Aren't you glad you came out on the boat?"

He returned a half smile and said, "I hate to admit it, but yeah, you're right. This time."

We laughed as she pulled out her phone from the back pocket of her shorts. "Photo time. I want to remember this day."

Macon and I stood behind her at the boat console. "Say 'Islanders!'" She clicked. "Perfect!" Lovie tucked the phone into her pocket and headed back to the console. "Sit down, guys. We're taking off."

After a few minutes of racing along the shoreline of Dewees Island, we spotted the very last house on a section of the island. Lovie slowed the engines and came to a stop. We bobbed in the water, staring at the remote house that seemed to jut out into the sea, dark and foreboding.

"That's Scary Harry's house," Lovie said.

"It's as creepy from the water as it is from the land," I said.

Macon added, "But it's an odd shape." He tilted his head in study.

I stood beside him, staring at the eerie house. Then I saw it. "It's like an old ship," I said. "See the point? That's the bow. And those small windows are the portholes."

"I see it," Lovie cried. "It'd be cool if it didn't belong to Scary Harry." The ocean breeze blew a clump of hair across Lovie's face.

Macon said with a groan, "Oh no. Guys! Look!"

Standing on the angled porch at the end of the house was a man. He was dressed in the same long-sleeved white shirt and khaki pants that we saw him wear on the beach. His white hair blew wildly around him as he peered out through binoculars.

"He looks like a ghost on the bow of an old ship," Macon said in a low voice.

"He's far away," I said. "He can't hear us. You don't have to whisper."

Just then, the old man moved the binoculars in our direction. "Duck!" Lovie cried.

We ducked low in the boat.

"He totally saw us!" I said, my heart pounding.

Macon peeked over the edge of the boat. "He's still looking right this way." He swung his head over to Lovie. "Get us out of here!"

She nodded and scrambled back to the boat console. "Sorry, Macon," she said as she turned the boat around.

"For what?" he asked.

"Just hold on tight!" She pushed the throttle forward and the boat sped away, making a rooster tail of water behind us.

"All clear!" Lovie called back.

Macon and I rose up off the deck of the boat with groans and took our seats on the bench. My blood was still coursing hard from the excitement. When Lovie turned around to look at us, we all burst into laughter.

"I think the guy has a sixth sense," Macon said. "It's like he zeros right in on us."

"I wondered if he thinks we're spying on him and his treasures," I said.

"Well, we were spying on him. Kind of," Macon said.

"We weren't doing anything wrong," Lovie said. "We were just out on a joyride and paused to look at his unusual house. Right?"

"Sure," said Macon with a smirk.

"I feel better now that we put some distance between us and Scary Harry's house," I said. "But I have to say, this trip has been awesome."

"Totally," Macon agreed. "But can you slow down now?"

He was gripping the side of the boat like a tree frog on a window.

Lovie's braid whipped behind her in the wind. "Oh gosh, yeah, sorry." She pulled back on the throttle. "I usually go this fast."

"No kidding," Macon said, and loosened his grip on the boat.

When she slowed down, the roar of the engine lessened and we felt the tension ease. We all sat back and enjoyed the feel of the sun on our faces and the occasional splash from the wake.

"This really has been the best day ever," Lovie said from the wheel. She turned her head toward us. "I missed us being together. Hanging out and having fun with you."

Macon and I looked at each other with meaning.

"What?" Macon said incredulously.

"*You're* the one who kept hanging out with those Island Invaders all summer," I said.

She swung her head around to glare at me. Turning back, she slowed down to a crawl, then turned off her engine. That done, Lovie turned around and faced us. She stood wide-legged for balance and crossed her arms.

Okay, I thought. *We're going to have it out. At last.*

"I was *not* hanging out with them. I was just doing what Honey asked."

"Like, every day?" I asked.

She didn't answer right away. When she spoke, her voice was so soft I had to lean forward to hear the words.

"You guys ditched me."

"No, we didn't," I replied, feeling defensive. "*You* ditched us. It's not like Honey asked you to be their best friend."

"I wasn't. It's called being *nice*."

"Yeah. If you say so." I looked off to see the green cordgrass waving in the wind.

"For the record," Macon said, "yes, you ditched us. Your *friends*." He emphasized his last word. "Being nice doesn't mean spending hours with the enemy. Every day."

"Well, *friends*"—Lovie spat out the word—"I feel like you excluded me. You guys were all buddy-buddy. Spying on me. Having a sleepover. Hoarding the metal detector. You made me feel like the odd one out." She paused. "You made me feel left out."

Lovie's voice wavered, and I hoped she wouldn't cry. I didn't think I could stand that.

"I'm sorry," I said.

"I'm sorry too," Macon said.

"We weren't The Islanders without you."

Lovie looked off at a passing boat. Its wake rippled across the water, rocking us when it hit. Then she turned to face us once again. I could see the glimmer of water in her eyes.

"That means a lot. Thanks, guys."

I sighed, glad we'd had this talk. Friendship was more than about having fun together. Real friendship was about loving each other enough to be honest with each other, help each other, be there when needed. I looked at Macon and Lovie, knowing they were my best friends.

"But, admit it," Macon said with a crooked smile. "You kind of did go overboard with those Invaders."

I groaned and jabbed Macon in the ribs. What did my dad say about letting go?

Lovie paused, and a small smile fluttered at her lips. "You're a little right this time, Macon," she admitted. "At first I thought I liked them. They were being super nice to me. But I soon saw them for what they really were. I thought maybe they were bored. But they looked for ways to cause trouble. They're not mean." She shrugged. "They're just real jerks." She straightened and turned back to the wheel. "I mean, who could take aim at a sweet little otter?"

CHAPTER 18

It's the alligator you don't see that's the most dangerous

B ACK ON THE GOLF CART, IT WAS TIME TO drop everyone off because dinnertime was getting close. Macon needed to get home first because of "big brother" duties, so we took the path that went past a part of the large pond. There were a ton of birds wading, and often a lot of gators, too.

"Hey, watch out, bro," Macon alerted us as he indicated a golf cart alongside the road. "I think that's Eddie's golf cart." He snorted. "Maybe they've taken up bird-watching."

I laughed.

"Yeah, sure," Lovie said with a giggle.

"Let's creep up on them," Macon suggested. "We've got a little time before I have to go home. I don't want to get stuck babysitting."

"So, this is what you guys did to me all summer?" Lovie asked with a pretend scowl.

"We cannot disclose information about our tactics," Macon said.

"Shhh," I said, trying to hold my own laughter. "We're spies, remember?"

"Well, you should know I saw you every single time," Lovie whispered.

"Did not," I replied.

"Shh." Lovie put her finger to her lips.

I parked my cart a good way behind theirs for a fast get-away. We hunched over and crept to the dock, careful to stay behind trees and bushes so they didn't see us.

I signaled for everyone to crouch down before peeking around the last tree. We were shielded by a big clump of palm fronds. Mosquitoes buzzed loudly near our ears, and sweat rolled down the sides of my face. The sun cut across the land from the west, shining right on us.

When I peeked through the foliage, a large grin spread across my face. On the low wooden platform that floated in the middle of the pond, there was Big Al. Resting in his favorite spot. A couple of other smaller gators rested at the edges with him, like courtiers for a king.

"It's Big Al," I whispered, signaling for them to take a look.

"And there are the Invaders," said Macon in a low voice. He pointed farther down by the edge of the pond. I spotted Eddie and Andy.

"They're just standing there," I said, wondering what they were up to.

I didn't have to wait long. Eddie pulled out a pebble from his fishing shirt pocket, then pulled out his slingshot from his back pocket.

"Oh no. Those idiots," Lovie whispered.

"What is it with this kid and his slingshot?" Macon said, shaking his head.

Eddie pulled back the strap of his slingshot, taking aim.

I saw where he was aiming. "Please tell me he's not going to . . ."

Before I could finish, Eddie released the strap. The small rock went sailing across the water straight toward the gator platform. It fell a few feet short of its target and made a small splash. One of the three smaller gators slipped into the water. Big Al didn't move.

Lovie clutched my arm. "He's going to do it again," she whispered with urgency. "This is so wrong! I'm stopping him."

She released my arm and stood up. Just then Andy launched a rock. I didn't even know he had a slingshot now too. We watched in horror as it arced over the pond to land with a splash near the gators.

The other two smaller gators slipped off the platform into the water. This time, Big Al's head moved.

Lovie scooted back down behind the foliage. "Uh-oh."

We heard the boys laugh again as another rock zinged into the air. A bigger rock making a longer arc. This one hit the platform just inches away from Big Al. It made a loud *thunk* on the wood, then bounced into the water with a noisy splash. This time, Big Al pushed his massive body off the platform and disappeared into the murky depths.

All the hairs on my body suddenly felt electrified. I could almost hear the *Jaws* movie theme music playing in my head. Eddie and Andy were laughing and high-fived each other.

Macon whispered with fear, "Where is Big Al?"

"It's the alligator you don't see that's the most dangerous," I whispered.

Lovie sprang out from behind the greens and yelled out to Eddie and Andy. "Run! Get out of there!"

Startled, the two boys swung around. Seeing Lovie, Eddie smiled.

"Hey, Lovie!" Eddie shouted back. "We're just shooting rocks in the pond."

"I'm not blind! You're aiming at the gators. You've scared Big Al off the dock. Get out of there. You weren't in danger when he was on the dock. Now we don't know where Big Al is!"

"Chill out, will you?" Andy slapped a mosquito at his ankle. "Ow!"

"Get out of there," I shouted at the top of my lungs. "Big Al is on the move!"

Just then, the water's edge exploded as one thousand pounds of alligator emerged from the pond to land on the bank with a roaring hiss. His enormous jaws were open, exposing rows of pointy teeth.

Andy and Eddie screamed, dropped their slingshots, turned heel, and ran for their lives. We ran as well. The echo of that explosive hiss seemed to radiate across the pond. I stopped at the road and held my arms out to halt Macon and Lovie.

"Wait!" I called out as they almost slammed into me. I swung around to look back toward the pond. "They're not going to make it to their golf cart."

Lovie and Macon stopped and looked over their shoulders. I could tell Macon was a breath away from sprinting to our golf cart.

As though they figured that out at the same time, Eddie and Andy jumped to grab a limb of a live oak tree, pulling themselves up. They climbed as fast as monkeys, as high up the tree as they could go.

To our relief, Big Al wasn't chasing the boys in anger. We watched as he ambled in his usual slow, plodding gait up the bank. There was no way the boys could outrun the alligator if Big Al saw them as prey. Nope. They were lucky Big Al didn't seem to be in any hurry.

Still, the alligator was on the move. Big Al lumbered toward the tree in his slow stride, dragging his long tail behind him. Back in the pond, the other gators lingered at the bank, as though watching the show.

"Alligators can't climb trees, can they?" asked Macon.

"I don't think so," Lovie said, her voice wobbling. "But I'm not sure. We need to get some help. We can't stay here and watch Big Al eat them!"

"They can't climb trees," I confirmed.

"How do you know?" Macon asked.

"I read it somewhere. Wait. Look," I said. "Big Al is moving past the tree."

We all sighed in relief as we watched Big Al lumber a few feet past the tree. Then he stretched his fourteen-foot body across the path and settled with a muffled thump onto the ground. He just sat there, his scaly sides expanding and contracting with each breath he took.

"He blocked their path out," Lovie said, wonderstruck. "Do you think he did that on purpose?"

"Yeah," both me and Macon said at the same time.

"Big Al is old," Macon said. "He's been around a long time. He knows what he's about."

"Help! Help!" Eddie and Andy yelled out from the tree.

"We'd better get Chief Rand," Lovie said.

"We'll go get help!" I yelled out. "Stay put!"

"Stop yelling," Macon said to us. "I don't want to be gator bait!"

We turned and hurried back to my golf cart, thankful I'd parked a distance away from the pond. Once in, I turned the cart around and headed back the way we came. I'd have to take the long way around the island because there was no way I was going to run up against Big Al in a bad mood. Lovie called island security on her cell phone as I sped back to the firehouse.

"Operation Rescue is on!" Macon called out.

CHAPTER 19

A dangerous situation

THE ISLAND'S FIRE TRUCK RACED TO THE scene. Chief Rand let us ride in the truck, and though it was exciting, I was disappointed he didn't turn on the siren. We climbed out and headed straight for the pond.

Chief Rand held out his arms. "Hold on, kids. This is a dangerous situation." His set face brooked no questions or disobedience. "There will be no running, no loud voices, and you children will stay a safe distance away. And if I tell you to get back to the truck, you go. No discussion. Understood?"

"Yes, sir," we all replied.

At Chief Rand's signal, we cautiously approached the tree

from the opposite side. My breath sucked in at seeing Big Al's fourteen-foot-long body lying still as a stone smack-dab in the middle of the path. He'd turned since we'd left. Now his long head was pointed at the tree where Eddie and Andy sat high up in the branches. They clung to the branches and stared down at the gigantic alligator with big eyes.

"Stalemate," declared Macon.

Chief Rand stood wide-legged, arms crossed, assessing the situation. "Correctomundo," he replied. "Well played, Big Al." Then he turned to us. "Kids, get comfortable. We have to wait this one out."

Honey and my dad drove up shortly after we did. They parked and hurried to join us at our vigil.

"Oh dear," Honey said when she saw the boys up in the tree. "The poor darlings. They must be terrified."

"What are they going to do?" I asked, wiping sweat off my head with my shirtsleeve.

"Nothing they can do right now," Honey said, pulling lightly at the front of her linen shirt, trying to keep cool. "There's no immediate threat or harm, other than this heat. I'm afraid we're on Al's time."

"Help! Please!" Eddie begged from his position crouched on a tree branch, with one arm around the trunk.

"Just shoot the alligator!" Andy cried out while swatting mosquitoes and clinging to the tree.

"That's not how we do it here, boys," Chief Rand called up to them. "The ecosystem has top predators for a reason, and you just wrangled with one." He shook his head. "Not smart. Now, just try to keep calm, boys. You're safe up there. We just have to wait it out. Big Al will move."

"How long?" Andy cried back.

Chief Rand crossed his arms. "As long as it takes, boys."

We clustered together close to the road, so as not to rile Big Al. When a golf cart approached, the people stopped to ask, "What's going on?" Chief Rand sent them on their way. "Big Al is blocking the path," he told them. "Best go around the other way." To us he explained, "We don't want a crowd upsetting Big Al right now."

I stood with my fellow Islanders, swatting mosquitoes, with our eyes glued to the tree while Big Al lorded over his territory. As much as I'd been angry at Eddie and Andy for shooting rocks at the gator, I felt bad seeing them so scared up in that tree.

Chief Rand put his fingers on the bridge of his nose and sighed in distress. He dropped his hand and shook his head wearily. "I don't get this," he said. "I've lived here all my life and I've never seen Big Al go after anyone. Not even a dog. Not once. This is bad news for Big Al."

"Why?" I asked.

"Because that there is a big bull. See, an alligator over four feet is considered a nuisance if it poses a threat to people. Truth is that alligators are naturally afraid of humans. If left alone, they'll move on. It's when folks feed them that they lose their fear of people. They get used to them and come closer. That's when they become a risk. Now, if it's a small gator, under four feet, in some states a nuisance will be relocated. You get a big old bull like Big Al here, and there's little tolerance for any misbehavior. Even if it's too comfortable interacting with people. That's why people shouldn't feed them. Any trouble at all and it'll have to be"—he glanced at us kids—"seriously removed."

"Relocated?" my dad asked.

Chief Rand met his gaze, then somberly shook his head. "No. In South Carolina, any nuisance alligator, especially one his size, is euthanized."

"You mean killed?" Lovie cried.

"I'm sorry, honey," Chief Rand said.

We all were rocked by the shock that Big Al could not only be taken away but killed.

Chief Rand rubbed his jaw in thought. "But here's what I don't understand. It's extremely rare for a gator to chase people. Big Al?" He shook his head. "I don't get it."

My dad walked to my side and patted my shoulder. "Did you see what happened?"

I looked at Macon and Lovie. In that shared look I understood that we didn't want to rat on the boys. But I couldn't lie to my dad. And we had to save Big Al.

"Yes, sir."

Chief Rand turned his head and gave me his full attention. "I'd appreciate it if you'd tell me what you saw." His gaze moved to Macon and Lovie. "All of you."

Lovie was the first to speak. "You can't kill Big Al," she

cried. "It wasn't his fault. The boys were throwing rocks at him. With slingshots."

Chief Rand's brows furrowed, and I saw his eyes spark. "Slingshots?"

"Yes, sir," I said, backing Lovie up. "We saw the boys' cart and we thought we'd check what they were up to." I looked at my feet. "See, they've been causing trouble all summer, and we've taken to . . . well . . . spying on them." I felt a blush heat my cheeks when I saw Chief Rand's lips twitch.

"Go on," Chief Rand said.

"They had their slingshots before," I told him. "They were shooting at birds."

"No!" exclaimed Honey.

"And an otter!" Lovie cried, still upset about that.

"We told them to stop." My hands balled up at my thighs.

"Yeah. We almost got in a fight about it," added Macon.

Dad asked, "Why didn't you tell us about the slingshots then?"

I looked at my feet again and shrugged. "We told them not to use them. And they couldn't hit anything, anyway. I guess we didn't want to rat them out."

"Did the boys use their slingshots to shoot rocks at Big Al?" asked Chief Rand. He was using his fire chief voice, the one that was calm but let you know he meant business.

"Yes, sir."

"I screamed at them to stop," Lovie said, her voice high. "But they just laughed. They kept firing at him. The other gators slid into the water and *still* they didn't stop. Big Al tried to ignore them," she said, her voice breaking. "They just didn't stop."

"And Big Al," continued Chief Rand. "What did he do?"

Lovie swallowed. "He left the platform, swam over, and hissed at them."

"Boy did they run," I said, not laughing. "I was worried they wouldn't get away. But Big Al didn't run after them. He kind of did his usual walk. You know, slow and steady. The boys climbed up the tree super fast, but he didn't menace them or anything like that. He just went and sat down on the path like he always does."

Chief Rand blew out a long stream of air. "Thanks, kids. That just might help out our favorite alligator a lot. It doesn't sound like he was being a nuisance after all. He was just defending himself." He looked out toward the pond. "Can you direct me to where those slingshots might be?"

When the sun sank behind the tree line, the stuffy heat was a little more bearable.

Without any obvious reason, Big Al pushed up slowly onto his massive legs and began his long, slow trek back to the pond.

From our vantage point, we held our breath, thrilled the big gator was heading back home. Big Al walked past the tree where Eddie and Andy still cowered, but he didn't pause. He just kept on walking, dragging his long tail behind him. Reaching the water, he soundlessly slid into the pond, disappearing beneath the dark surface.

Chief Rand and his team sprang to action. They brought the fire truck closer to the tree and, using their ladders, at last rescued the boys. By now their parents had arrived, and the boys ran into their arms.

I watched as a Department of Natural Resources officer walked over to the boys and their parents. In his hands he was holding the slingshots.

"Show's over," said Honey. "Time to go home."

"What's going to happen now?" I asked Honey as we all walked back to our carts.

"Well, it's illegal to harass alligators. So I am guessing that the nice DNR officer over there will be writing them both a

hefty fine." She clucked her tongue. "Could be up to a couple of thousand dollars."

Macon released a long, slow whistle.

"Will they have to go to court or anything?" Lovie asked.

Honey shrugged. "Ain't my business, but"—she looked at the three of us and gave a mischievous grin as she swatted a mosquito from her arm—"I'm guessing their time up that tree will be punishment enough."

CHAPTER 20

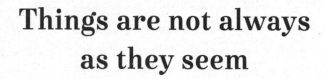

Things are not always as they seem

THE NEXT DAY, WHILE I WAS HANGING OUT at the Nature Center with my friends, Honey shocked us with some news.

"Listen up, children. We have a date this evening. I'll need all of you to be dressed nicely and at my house at exactly seven o'clock."

I looked up from my journal, where I was recording all the events with Big Al. We kids had to repeat our story to the Department of Natural Resources official, but it was worth all the trouble. Big Al was given a reprieve. The officials decided the alligator wasn't being aggressive but was instead willfully attacked by the two boys and their slingshots. Eddie and Andy left the island today. Good riddance. We weren't eager to see them return. The whole experience gave me an idea for a short story. I even had a title: "Big Al's Revenge."

"Where are we going?" Lovie asked Honey.

"We've been invited to Mr. Maynard's house. Your dad asked him to take a look at your coins."

Lovie dropped her book, and Macon nearly fell backward in his chair.

"You want us to go to Scary Harry's house?" Macon asked, shocked.

"No way, Honey," I said, shaking my head. "He's creepy."

Honey narrowed her eyes and put her hands on her hips. "Y'all can quit calling him that name. His name is Mr. Harold Maynard." She paused and clasped her hands together like she was about to give us a lesson.

"Let me teach you something, children. Things are not always as they seem." She reached down and picked up my black-and-white composition notebook. "For example, look at this notebook," she said. "You can go to the store and buy one just like it for under one dollar. It's nothing special. Some kids put stickers on it or draw a picture and mess it all up. If you see a notebook like this on someone's desk, you don't think much about it. It's just for taking notes, or whatever. But ... when I open up this notebook ..." She opened it, and I cringed at seeing my pages exposed. "Look at the beautiful drawings inside. And all the descriptions. Even stories."

She gave me back my journal. "Nice job," she said, then reached for Lovie's. "Oh, and see? This one is completely different. It's full of photographs." She handed it back to Lovie with, "They're beautiful, dear."

When she reached for Macon's, he grabbed it and pulled back. Honey smiled. "That's okay, Macon. Some people put personal information in their notebooks. It's important to respect privacy. My point is, each of your journals looks the same on the outside. They're just common, cheap notebooks. But open them up, and they are as wonderfully different and creative as you are. It's the same with people. You don't know much by looking at the outside. It's what's inside that matters."

We all sat silent. Lovie was fiddling with her turtle necklace and Macon was pursing his lips in thought.

"And yes, we are going," Honey said in conclusion. "I've already talked with your mama, Macon. And Sissy gave her approval too. Now stop acting like this is a punishment. Do you want to learn about those coins you found or not?"

Macon showed up exactly at seven o'clock. He had on a preppy, green gingham button-down shirt, white shorts, and brand-new-looking sneakers.

"You look like you snatched that off a store mannequin," I teased him. Truth was, I was impressed by his sense of style.

He punched me in the arm as he walked in. "Well, at least I don't look like my grandma dressed me!"

I looked down at my ironed khaki pants and light purple,

short-sleeve polo shirt. "What's the matter with my clothes?"

"Dude. Lavender?"

I had to laugh. "Yeah, I hate the color purple too."

Now he laughed and playfully socked my arm. "Cheer up. I bet Lovie will think you're cute."

My cheeks flamed. "Whatever." I punched him back, and hard enough to make him stop laughing.

"Okay, okay . . ." He rubbed his arm but still was grinning.

Five seconds later, Lovie arrived wearing a tropical-looking sundress. Her hair wasn't in the usual braid. It was loose and wavy in a way I'd never seen before. We both stared at her.

"Hey! Don't you two clean up well," she said at the doorway. She slid between us and lifted her phone. "Selfie!" she called out, and snapped a picture with her phone.

"Hey!" Macon protested. "You didn't even give us a heads-up."

"I was going for the natural look," she said, checking the photo. "Don't worry, you look great." She held out her phone screen to show us. As I leaned in to see, I thought she smelled like peaches and coconut. Two things I really liked.

"I like your shirt, Jake," Lovie said as she strolled off to the kitchen.

Macon elbowed me, grinning. I made a face behind her back.

"Do you have the coins?" Lovie asked as she plucked a grape off a stem.

I jiggled my pocket. "Got 'em."

"Doesn't it feel weird that we're doing this?" Macon asked. "I mean, look at us. We're all dressed up to meet the creepiest guy on the island."

"But we really want to know about the history of these coins. We gotta do what we gotta do," Lovie said with a drawl.

Macon slumped his shoulders. "Yeah, you're right. But it still feels totally weird." He stuffed a cracker in his mouth.

Dad walked into the kitchen. "Okay, gang. Ready to go?"

He had a freshly shaved face and combed hair. But it was his clothes that made my eyes widen. "Uh, Dad . . . we're twins."

He looked pointedly at my outfit, then back at his outfit.

"Note to self," he said. "Never, I mean ever, let Honey go clothes shopping for us."

"I think it's kinda cute." Lovie giggled. "Matching outfits."

Macon silently shook in laughter, while I wished I were a gator and could just quietly sink to the bottom of a pond.

"My, my!" Honey breezed into the kitchen, wearing a bright yellow sundress, lipstick, and a big turtle necklace. "Don't my boys look handsome!" She kissed Dad on the cheek, leaving a kiss print on his cheek.

"Thanks, Mom." Dad shrugged and made a face that only we could see.

"Lovie, dear," Honey said. "You look very pretty tonight too. Could you take a photo of me with my favorite guys? All of us dressed up is quite the rare sight." She called us to stand right beside her.

Dad and I groaned but obliged her request.

"Oh, you all look fabulous. This is going to be such fun!" Honey grabbed an insulated container that carried her mixed berry pie, then looked at us with confusion. "Why the long faces? We're going on an adventure!"

CHAPTER 21

The thrill of the hunt

MACON AND LOVIE RODE IN MY CART AS we followed Dad's single file. Dad's cart turned in to the driveway with the sign that read HAROLD MAYNARD, DEWEES ISLAND, SC. I stopped my cart. Us kids gave one another a knowing look. Then, taking a deep breath, I drove forward. As we made our way up his long, winding driveway, our nerves kept us silent.

The house loomed ahead of us, shadowy in the dim light. The roofline jutted skyward at sharp angles. I expected to see a gargoyle guarding the door. Up close, the wood was so dark and aged, it appeared black. Lights shone from inside the house, and by the large wooden front door hung a huge brass lantern that looked like it had been ripped from a great ship.

And there he stood, wide-legged on a sweeping, curved porch that stretched across the entire front of the dark wooden house.

"You think he knows that was us on the boat yesterday?" Macon asked in a low voice.

"Maybe. You think he's going to say something about it?" I asked, worried.

Lovie toyed with her necklace. "Y'all are acting like a bunch of scaredy cats. We were just boating. Let's go. Honey's giving us the stink eye." She slid off the cart and strode toward the house without looking back.

I took a deep breath and tried to fake some courage as we followed her up the creaky steps toward Scary Harry.

"Harold, how nice of you to invite us." Honey greeted Scary Harry warmly, handing him the pie box. "Hope you like berry pie."

"What's this for?" he said, looking puzzled.

"Just a token of thanks for making time for us today."

"What?" He pointed at his ear. "I can't hear you. Speak up."

I could see a hearing aid peeking out of his ear.

Honey cleared her throat and spoke louder. "I said, I hope you like berry pie."

A look of surprise slowly replaced his hardened look. "My favorite. How'd you know?" He reached out to accept the pie. I sucked in my breath at seeing the missing tips of his fingers. "Come in," he said, and turned toward the house with an extended arm. "Please." Then he turned toward us. "You coming?"

We looked at one another, then hurriedly followed the adults into the house.

Inside, it was kind of dark too. But not in a creepy way. It was, in fact, very cool. I looked around, and to my surprise, I found myself smiling in awe. I felt like I'd walked onto a ship. One time in California, my parents took me on board the *Queen Mary*. This house reminded me of that great ship. Scary Harry's walls were also all wood, gleaming with what Honey would call a spit shine. The stair railings, light fixtures, and door handles were all made of shiny brass.

Honey turned to introduce the rest of us. "Harold, I suspect your paths might have crossed over the years. My son was raised here on Dewees. But I'd like you to formally meet my son, Eric. He is a retired Army captain."

Scary Harry set the pie box down, straightened, and reached out for a handshake with his scarred hand and the missing tips of his fingers. I wondered if he had any idea that my dad was missing the lower part of his leg, undetectable in long pants.

"I served in the Army too," Harold said. "I volunteered in July 1965. As soon as I was eighteen, I signed up. Served four years."

"Vietnam, I assume?" Dad asked.

The old man nodded slowly. "Yep. Lost a lot of really good men out there."

Dad lowered his head. "I understand. All too well."

Honey turned toward me next. "And, Harold," she said loud enough for him to hear, "these wonderful children are my grandson, Jake, and his friends Lovie Legare and Macon Simmons."

He looked at us with his narrow, pale eyes. Mr. Maynard had only one word for all of us. "Hello."

Macon stepped toward the man to say, "Thank you for your service, sir," and then backstepped.

Lovie gave a small wave. "Nice to meet you, sir."

I had to muster up the nerve to reach out a hand. "Thank you for having us over."

Harold Maynard took my hand and gave it a quick pump. His skin was dry and his fingers bony, but it was not scary.

"I believe we've met before," he said with a smile in his voice.

I paled.

When no one spoke, the old man smiled. "On the beach. I'm the old codger with the metal detector."

We all mumbled, "Oh yes," while nodding our heads.

"Find anything interesting?" he asked. "Beside soda cans and tabs?" He chuckled. "Let me give you all a tour. I spent years perfecting this house. It's pretty much my world." He looked out the vast picture window that overlooked the ocean. "This and the beach."

He walked in his stooped, slow gait, but I could still feel his pride as he guided us from stern to bow of his incredible boat on land. We ended up at a narrow point that poked out through the trees toward the ocean. Overhead was a row of small windows that looks like portholes.

"This is what we saw from the boat," I whispered to Macon. He nodded but didn't speak.

"I designed all this myself," Mr. Maynard said. He led us to the open living room. "You know," he added with a chuckle, "I haven't had guests in quite some time." He smiled and looked over his shoulder at us. "It's nice." He spread out his arms. "Look around at anything you'd like."

Macon headed straight for a side table that was really a large ship's compass. I wandered over to an old painting of ships that was so large it took up half a wall. The painting depicted a great battle on the rough high seas. Several ships had their cannons spewing smoke. One ship had a small, tattered Jolly Roger flag flying.

"Pirates," I whispered to myself.

"Whoa! This is incredible." Lovie was bent over a cabinet, and her breath was fogging up the glass.

Mr. Maynard drew near and rubbed the fog from the glass case top with his sleeve. "It's a replica of the *Queen Anne's Revenge*. It cost me quite a few gold doubloons to get this model of ol' Blackbeard's ship. Do you like it?"

Macon whistled softly as he nodded.

"Come this way," Mr. Maynard said, leading us toward another case. He tapped on the case with his damaged finger. "I think you'll be interested in these." He cast a searching gaze across the three of us. "These are my real treasures. The ones I found myself. Some I found right here on Dewees Island. Others"—his lips curled, and he shrugged his bony shoulders—"elsewhere in the world."

We clustered closer to peer into the glass case. Each item was carefully displayed on black velvet with a sign of information below it.

"Oh, look at the buttons," Lovie said, pointing. "It says they're from before the Civil War."

Macon leaned far over the glass. "These musket balls are cool." He turned to Mr. Maynard. "Did you find these with your metal detector?"

"Yes, I did."

Macon smiled and nodded his head. "I've got to find me some of those."

I looked down at a collection of old bottles in different sizes, shapes, and colors, mostly deep blue, emerald green, or brown. And next to that, I saw coins. My breath caught. I pointed to one large gold coin separated from the rest.

"This one," I blurted out. "Is this the one I saw in the newspaper? The gold doubloon?"

Macon and Lovie scurried closer to get a better look at the gold coin that had sparked our own search for treasure.

Mr. Maynard approached with his hands behind his back. He smiled, and it transformed his face from harsh to kind. "The very one," he replied. "And the greatest find of my career."

I couldn't wait any longer. I pulled out the coins we'd found in Dad's old treasure box and thrust them toward Scary Harry. "Mr. Maynard, do you know what these coins are?"

He held out his palm for the coins. He bent over them in study, and when he straightened, it seemed his eyes were dancing with excitement.

"Very interesting. Let's have a closer look, shall we? Follow me."

We followed him down the hall to a different room. He pushed open the heavy wooden doors.

"Oh my," exclaimed Honey as we entered, and she put her hand to her chest. The walls were floor to ceiling shelves, each filled to the brim with books. A long, rolling ladder was attached to a brass rail. I couldn't imagine old Mr. Maynard climbing up that tall ladder to fetch a book. But he must have, because there was no one else living in the house. I could tell Honey was in book heaven.

We followed Mr. Maynard to a large antique desk in the corner that was as big as our dining room table. Even so, the top was littered with papers. Clicking on a small green lamp atop the desk, he took a seat and laid the coins out on the leather top. While Honey wandered the room devouring the books with her eyes, us kids clustered around the desk, our eyes wide with anticipation. Dad took an empty chair close by. We were so quiet we could hear the old man's heavy breathing.

He picked up his magnifying glass with his bony hands and leaned over the coins. His longish wispy hair fell forward as he studied them. After a few minutes he swiveled in his chair to reach out for a book farther away on his desk. Thumbing through it, he made notations on a piece of paper. He did this over and over again, filling up a page with notes.

My feet were beginning to ache from standing. At last, he leaned back in his chair and turned to look at us.

We all straightened.

"Well, children, this is a mighty lucky find."

I cleared my throat. "To be honest, sir, *we* didn't exactly find the coins. Not originally. My dad did. Back when he was a kid."

Mr. Maynard turned to my father. "You did?"

"Yes, sir. Me and Chief Rand."

"When?"

Dad blew out a plume of air. "I reckon it was some time in the early 1990s."

"Where?"

"Out on the beach, here on Dewees." Dad cracked a smile. "Me and Rand were hunting for Blackbeard's treasure."

Mr. Maynard chuckled. "Indeed."

"Is it pirate treasure?" asked Macon, his voice cracking.

Mr. Maynard shook his head. "I'm afraid not, my boy." When Macon's face fell, he held up his hand. "Don't be disappointed. These coins may have come from a sunken ship."

We all leaned forward, eyes wide. "Really?"

He nodded and reached over to pick up one of the coins. "Unless I'm wrong—and I'm never wrong—these coins came from a big vessel that sank off these shores back in 1801. A schooner." He smiled ruefully. "There's not much information out there about the vessel. I know, because I've looked." He leaned forward to rest his elbows on the desk and steepled his fingers. Then he looked at us. His eyes were shining. "It sank with a cargo load full of coins and other valuables. Right off the coast of Dewees Island."

We all exhaled. Wow, I couldn't believe it. Dewees Island!

"It is said to have been carrying a real treasure," Mr. Maynard continued.

"Well, I'll be darned," said Dad with a look of wonder on his face.

Mr. Maynard leaned back in his chair. "I've been searching for that treasure for the better part of fifty years." He shook his head and laughed again. "And you walk into my house carrying three of these coins." He laughed again. "Isn't life full of surprises?"

"How much do you think they're worth?" I asked. I crossed my fingers.

Mr. Maynard studied me a moment. "Well, I'll tell you this. Some coins in pristine condition like this could be worth hundreds, maybe thousands of dollars each."

He scooted to the edge of his chair.

We stepped closer.

"But what you've got here are Spanish coins, dated from about 1800. They're not especially rare. The monetary value might not be what you hoped for."

"How much?" Macon asked.

Mr. Maynard paused, then said with a slight shrug, "Maybe fifty bucks. Each."

My heart sank like a boat anchor. "Oh."

"That's more than I thought they'd be worth," Dad said.

"Don't get all down in the dumps about it. It's still a great find. Better than garbage on the beach, eh?" Mr. Maynard said, as he fidgeted with one of his hearing aids.

I rocked on my heels and tried to muster enthusiasm. "Sure, I guess."

Macon and Lovie were also slump-shouldered, leaning against the desk.

Mr. Maynard slapped his hand on his desk, causing us all to jump up.

"Now, listen to me, child." His gaze moved to include Lovie and Macon. "Children." Mr. Maynard's lips curved upward, and his gaze softened. "I've been doing this for a long time. A long, long time," he added with a sigh. "Sometimes you find something interesting, like those musket balls. Sometimes you find a small piece of history, like a fragment of Native American pottery. And I tell you . . ." He looked up at the ceiling and smiled. "You feel as lucky as if you've uncovered a dinosaur." He sighed and spread out his palms. "But most of the time, you find the tab of a soda can."

We all chuckled at that, Macon especially.

"So why do I go out day after day? For the money? Nah," Mr. Maynard said with a dismissive wave of his hand. "I'm an old man. How much money do I need? I'll tell you what keeps me going out." His voice rose with fervor. "It's the thrill of the hunt!" He slapped his knee for emphasis. "Yes, sir. Ain't nothing like it." He paused and looked at his hands. Then he held them out for us to look at. "See these fingers? I lost those fingertips back in Vietnam. Got my scars in an explosion. I suffered, sure, but I'm glad to be alive." He looked at my dad for a long moment, and my dad nodded his head in silent acknowledgment.

"Thrill of the hunt," Mr. Maynard repeated. "Every day I wake up and first, I'm grateful I woke up!" He chuckled softly to himself. "Then I wonder, what surprise will I discover today?" He paused. "Hope, children. That's the real treasure. I promise you."

He squinted his eyes at all of us, then slapped his hand hard on the table again. "Don't *ever* lose sight of that!"

CHAPTER 22

True friends are the
best treasure

AS JULY ROLLED INTO AUGUST, TURTLE nest hatches were keeping the Dewees Island Turtle Patrol busy. This late in the season the mother turtles had finished nesting and returned to the sea. Nests were emerging at night under the cloak of darkness. Mornings were filled with inventories of hatched nests. Inventories happened three days after the hatchlings emerged from the nest and scurried to the sea. The team opened the nest and counted the hatched and unhatched eggs. Every once in a while, they'd find trapped hatchlings in the nest. They rescued them, and we all got the chance to watch the tiny three-inch hatchlings scramble madly across the beach toward the sea and home.

Honey roped me into being the counter of eggs at the nest inventories. Waking up and getting to the beach in time for Dawn Patrol was tough, but worth it. Every time Turtle Patrol volunteers opened up a nest that had hatched, it felt to me like they were opening a treasure chest. You didn't know what you'd find. *The thrill of the hunt.*

I liked helping because I got to see Lovie, too. I'd missed spending a lot of time with her this summer because of the stupid Invader boys. I was glad to have a chance to make up for lost time. I knew summer was winding down and before long we'd be packing up and leaving Dewees Island for another year of school.

I looked over to see Lovie taking photographs of the hatchlings in Honey's red plastic bucket. There were seven discovered trapped in the roots of sea oats. Two of them had twisted shells from the roots growing up tight around them during their incubation in the egg. Lovie's long braid fell over her shoulder as she bent over the bucket. Her skin was deeply tanned after the summer outdoors. In the morning sun, her hair appeared almost white. My heart flip-flopped, and I thought of what Macon told me. *She likes you.*

Later that evening, Honey baked a chocolate cake and invited my friends over to the house to celebrate the end of our summer. We gathered on the porch, where she had the chocolate cake and plates at the ready.

Macon whistled when he saw it. "Wow. Nice setup. Whose birthday is it?"

Honey laughed. "No one's. But I believe that life's moments should be celebrated. It's been another wonderful summer, and we soon must say goodbye. Isn't that enough reason for cake?"

"I don't think we need a reason for cake," I said, licking my lips, ready for a slice.

"That's my boy," Honey said with a gentle pat to my cheek. She pointed over to her small cooler. "Grab yourself a cold drink."

Macon dug out a canned soda and sat down by Dad and Lucky. He reached out and pet the dog, rubbing behind his ears, causing his foot to start tapping. The porch door slid open, and Lovie stepped inside. She was wearing a pink polka-dot blouse over her jean cutoffs, not her usual T-shirt. I did a double take. In her hands, she held a wrapped present.

"Hey, y'all!" She smiled brightly, and everyone greeted her back.

"For me?" I teased, looking at the wrapped box. "You shouldn't have."

She held the box out to me. "Actually, there's something in here for you. And Macon," she hurried to add.

I wanted to swallow my words. "Uh, thanks," I said, and took the box. I shook it and pretended to listen to what was inside.

"Can we open it now?" Macon called out from his seat. Lucky was now stretched out across his lap.

"If you want," Lovie answered coyly.

I looked down at the box, wrapped in colorful paper, and tugged at the twine bow. Then I passed it over to Macon. "You can rip off the wrapping paper."

"Sure thing." Macon shifted in his seat, making Lucky jump from his lap. He tore the paper off the box and lifted the lid. Inside there were two thin white books. Looking closer I could read the black lettering on the front. In all caps it read MEMORIES. Under this, the next line read THE ISLANDERS. Macon looked up at Lovie, not sure what to do next.

"You each get one," Lovie said.

"Oh." Macon handed one to me.

"What is this?" I asked as we each slowly opened a book.

Lovie sat next to me on the wooden bench.

"This is my journal," she said. "I put all the photos I took of our summer together. They're both the same." She watched us go through a few more pages, then blurted, "I hope you guys like it."

"This is"—Macon said, slowly turning pages—"the coolest gift I've ever gotten."

Lovie put her hands to her cheeks, smiling. "Really?"

"Yeah. You caught so many things." He laughed and pointed to one picture. "You even got a shot of Scary Harry and his metal detector."

"And there's one of you with *your* metal detector."

Macon looked at Lovie with a smirk. "I noticed you put the pictures side by side. A comparison study, maybe?"

She giggled and shook her head. "No, I just grouped the

metal detector shots. But that would've been a good idea."

On page after page there were photos of the animals and plants she spied this summer, our favorite places on the island, like the gazebo, Huyler House, the Nature Center, us in my golf cart. There were so many of us, together and smiling.

"I'm not much of a writer, like you," Lovie said, looking at me. "And I can't draw like you, Macon. But I love photography." She pulled her braid onto her shoulder. "So I thought I'd make a photo journal . . . of us."

I stopped at the page with a large photograph of us in front of the old tree fort on the day we found the treasure box. We were sweaty and dirty and smiling. We were together. She had typed the date beneath the photo and captioned it *True friends are the best treasure.*

I turned my head. Lovie was sitting so close beside me, I could see the freckles smattered across her nose. Her blue eyes searched mine, wondering, hoping, that I liked her gift. I liked it a lot. And I liked her. But I couldn't speak those words.

"This is . . . incredible," I said. "Really great."

She smiled and it lit up her face. "I'm so glad."

The sound of a text message alert pinged on Honey's cell phone. "Get that for me, will you," Honey said to me, cutting into the cake.

"It's from Chief Rand," I said.

Honey paused from placing cake on plates to look up. "He doesn't ever message me. Must be important." She put a slice onto a plate. "Read it to me, please."

I read the text aloud.

I apologize for this late notice.

I need you, Eric, Macon, Lovie, and Jake at the boat landing.

Pronto. Important.

I looked up from the phone message, eyes wide. The last time Chief Rand called us out at night was when we got in big trouble for stealing a boat.

Honey frowned. "That's weird. What's so important at nine-thirty at night?"

"Are we in trouble or something?" I asked cautiously. Then I groaned. "Does this have anything to do with Eddie and Andy?"

Honey handed Dad his cake. "That can't be possible. Those boys are long gone. Off the island. That problem is tied up in a box and set high on the shelf." She looked at her watch. "Eat up. Guess we better follow orders."

Because it was dark, we all piled into one golf cart. My dad's was the biggest, so he drove. The three of us kids were squeezed together like sardines in the back seat. Lovie sat in the middle.

"I can't think of a single reason why Chief Rand needs us," Lovie wondered aloud.

Macon turned his head, and even in the dark I could see his eyes narrow in suspicion. "Did you guys do something I need to know about?"

"No way." Then I laughed and bumped shoulders. "Not this time." I heard Lovie giggle beside me.

We were quiet as we stared into the thick blackness. Only a sliver of the moon was visible. Out here on the island, with no streetlamps, away from the glow of suburbs and cities, it's a different kind of dark. As thick as velvet.

Suddenly, a tiny white light flashed to my right. I jerked my head to follow it. "Did y'all see that?"

Dad slowed to a stop and clicked off the headlights. "I saw it. Over there somewhere. Three o'clock."

It was so dark I couldn't see where he'd pointed. But then a tiny light blinked again. Within moments, there were several tiny lights floating around us, blinking on and off, over and over.

"Fireflies," Lovie crooned with delight.

"What are fireflies?" asked Macon.

Lovie looked at him with a surprised expression. "You know, lightning bugs."

"Uh, what?" Macon asked.

"I didn't see fireflies where I lived in New Jersey, either," I said. Maybe it was because we lived in the city. But I remembered seeing them here on Dewees Island when I was little. "Don't you have fireflies in Atlanta?"

"Nope. At least not any I've seen." He paused as a firefly lit up a few feet from us. "They sure are pretty."

Honey sighed. "I've always loved them. When I grew up, it seemed like fireflies were everywhere. Their numbers are decreasing. It's sad you've never seen one, Macon."

"But why are they disappearing?" Macon asked.

Dad laughed. "I reckon it's because of all of us kids who caught so many and put them in glass jars."

Honey laughed and slapped his shoulder. "Don't listen to him. Even if he did that. The simple truth is more development means destruction of woodlands and prairies. And that means loss of habitat." She smiled wistfully, "To me, fireflies have always been a sign of summer." She sighed. "Enjoy this, children. It's becoming more and more rare to see fireflies on summer nights."

We watched in awe as the soft glow flashed in different patterns all around us.

Honey remembered, "Oops! Captain Rand's waiting!"

As we took off again, Macon said in the darkness, "Y'all got some crazy bugs around here. Flying cockroaches and bugs that light up!"

Only one light guided us to the Dewees Island Ferry dock. Chief Rand stood waiting, wide-legged with his arms crossed. He lifted one powerful arm in a wave. Dad waved back.

"He's not wearing his uniform," I said in a low voice to Macon and Lovie as we climbed from the golf cart.

"That's got to be a good sign," Macon said.

"Thanks for meeting me out here on short notice," said Chief Rand.

Lovie blurted out, "Are we in trouble?"

Chief Rand threw his head back, laughing. "No. Sorry if

I scared you. There's just something important I want to show you."

The three of us sighed in relief.

"What's so important that you needed to drag us down to the dock at nine-thirty at night?" asked Honey.

"Better be good," Dad joked. "You made me miss out on cake."

"Oh, this will be worth it." Chief Rand smiled crookedly and said, "Just follow me."

We tended to obey orders from Chief Rand. In single file we followed him down the long, narrow dock to the floating platform. Tonight, the ferry was out. The only boats there were Lovie's little red boat and a bigger boat that I recognized as Chief Rand's. He waved us closer.

"Watch this," Chief Rand said.

I couldn't figure out what he was up to when he lowered and stretched out to lie flat on his stomach. Macon turned to me and lifted his hands in a *What's up?* gesture. I shook my head and shrugged.

"You okay there, buddy?" asked Dad with a chuckle.

"Just wait," Chief Rand called back.

Honey sucked in her breath and cooed. "Oh, I know what this is about."

Chief Rand stretched his arm down to the water. Curious, we drew closer, forming a semicircle around him. The ocean water was midnight blue, and I wondered if there was some exotic fish or crab he wanted us to see.

Chief Rand slowly ran his fingers across the inky water.

I gasped. What happened? A swirl of white sparks swirled around his fingers. When he moved his hand in a swoosh through the water, the surreal color followed it along with white sparkles.

Lovie squealed. "What *is* that?"

Macon dropped to his knees to get closer. "It's like science fiction. This can't be real!" His voice cracked with excitement.

Chief Rand turned his head with a smug smile. "Oh, it's real, all right."

Macon dipped his hand into the water and swished it across the surface. He laughed aloud when it looked like tiny sparkles were shooting out from his fingertips.

Lovie and I scrambled to lie on either side of Macon. We couldn't wait to try our hands at this magic. My dad lay beside me. In a row on the dock, flat on our bellies, side by side, we laughed and giggled as we splashed the ocean water with our hands.

"It looks like the sparks you see when something metal strikes concrete, hard and fast," I said.

"It looks like fairies to me," said Lovie.

Rand said, "It's called bioluminescence."

"Bio-lu-me what?" I asked.

Honey sat down next to Dad, putting her feet in. When she kicked at the water, the blue-green light swirled wildly.

"Bioluminescence is a chemical emission of light by organisms that live in the sea."

"Would you like to explain that so we can understand it?" Dad teased her.

Honey kicked a slight spray of sparkling water toward her son. "Well, now… In the oceans there are thousands of creatures that glow with light. They produce it themselves. The kind that we see now live here year-round. But in the summer, when there are lots of them, they emit light when they're disturbed." She kicked, and again we saw the otherworldly, swirling sparkles.

"Is it like the fireflies we saw tonight?" I asked.

"Yes, exactly!"

"Thanks for the science lesson, Mom."

She laughed. "You're welcome."

"I love this," Macon said, awestruck. "I never saw this before. Not ever. I never even knew this kind of thing existed."

"I know," I said. "It's magic."

"Who needs magic?" asked Honey. "We have nature."

Chief Rand rose and dusted off his belly. "Speaking of nature, I thought this would be a perfect night to really get a good look at Mother Nature. Who's ready for a boat ride?"

Lovie and I called out, "We are!"

Macon mumbled, "Not me. I'm having fun right here."

"Come with us," I told Macon. "We can't leave you here alone. We're The Islanders. It's one of our last nights here. We do things together, right?"

Macon turned his head and looked at me. I could see he was taking my words to heart. "Fine."

Chief Rand waited until we all stood. Macon was the last. He didn't want to stop playing with the water.

Chief Rand stepped closer to Dad, who was slowly bringing his leg into position to stand. Rand offered him a hand. "Here you go, pal."

My stomach clenched. I knew my dad didn't like to be offered help.

"Thank you." Dad reached out to take Rand's hand. With a firm hoist, Dad was on his feet again.

Chief Rand put an arm around Dad's shoulder. "I hope you don't mind. I have a guest."

He turned toward the boat. "Want to come out and say hello?"

We all stared at the boat as a slight woman's figure came to the edge. Chief Rand extended his hand to help her hop to the dock. Lovie and I looked at each other with wide eyes. Chief Rand had a girlfriend?

Something about the way she looked, the way she walked . . . When she drew closer, I saw a face illuminated in the moonlight. I couldn't believe it.

"Mom!" I cried, and ran to her. I slammed into her and wrapped my arms around her waist. She was laughing. I was crying. She held me tight. I held her tighter.

"I wanted to surprise you," she told me.

"You sure did," I said, my voice muffled against her shoulder. I inhaled the scent of her.

When I moved aside, I saw Dad standing beside us. He was looking at my mother and she was looking at him in that

way that I knew they felt they were the only two people in the world. I stepped aside, giving them some privacy.

"This is so romantic," Lovie said, sidling up to me.

I wiped the tears from my face, grateful it was such a dark night.

"Did you know?" Macon asked.

I shook my head. "No."

"Best surprise ever," Macon decided.

The adults clustered together talking and laughing. I knew that could take a while, so I walked back to the edge of the dock and lay again on my belly. In a flash Macon was on my right. Then Lovie lowered herself to my left.

"I wonder if this is how the glow stick got invented," Macon said. "Like one night he was kicking around in the water, saw all this, then went back to his lab to create instant bioluminescence in a tiny tube."

We laughed. "Maybe," I replied.

"I know it's science," Lovie said. "But to me, it's still magic. You know?"

She yawned and rested her head against my shoulder.

Macon yawned noisily and glanced my way. Seeing Lovie's head on my shoulder, he mouthed, *I told you so.* I didn't move. I didn't speak. I didn't want this moment to end.

I thought again about how we'd all be leaving Dewees soon. But I couldn't dwell on that. Not on a night like this. Not one so full of the magic of nature.

The three of us lay side by side on the dock, our arms

dangling to let our fingers create magic in the water. We swirled our hands in the warm water. It felt like we were playing with the Milky Way. It felt right. "Hey, Islanders," I called out. "What will our next adventure be?"

ACKNOWLEDGMENTS

THIS STORY IS ABOUT A SEARCH FOR TREA-
sure. The children discover that the greatest treasures
are not made of gold or silver but are found in their
relationships with their family, friends, and the natural world.
We have also discovered such treasures as we wrote this book
and would like to try, however ineptly, to express our gratitude.

Our Team

We are blessed to have the A team on our side. As corny as it
sounds, and we like corny, you are the wind beneath our sails.
There is so much we can say and still the words are inade-
quate. It takes a lot of cooperation to send a series out to the
world, and we are so grateful that we work seamlessly
together. Please know that in these pat phrases our senti-
ments run deep.

At Aladdin Books, sincere gratitude to:

Alyson Heller, our fabulous editor. Sincere thanks for

Acknowledgments

making writing for this audience a joy and a continuing learning experience. We are so thankful for your sensitivity and spot-on edits, and your humor is appreciated. Our first two books have been such a delight to work on with you. Thank you!

Jennifer Bricking, whose artwork for the series is fresh and imaginative. We both feel we hit the jackpot with your illustrations! The Islanders and Big Al thank you!

Valerie Garfield, who took a chance on our story of a brave boy and his best friends who will help teach children the joy of unplugging and enjoying the natural world.

For all your support of The Islanders series, we are sincerely grateful to *Nicole Russo, Laren Carr, Michelle Leo, Amy Beaudoin, Sarah Woodruff, Alissa Nigro, Anna Jarzab,* and *Nadia Almahdi.*

The Home Team, love and heartfelt thanks to:

Faye Bender, The Book Group, your knowledge of middle-grade and your savvy about the publishing world have helped us create this happy collaboration and guided us with both the writing and the business sides of middle-grade fiction. We are eternally grateful.

Kathie Bennett, Magic Time Literary and Publicity, your relationships and sterling reputation have placed The Islanders series in the hands of bookstores, schools, and academies, and for this and so much more we are forever grateful.

Laura Rossi, Laura Rossi PR, you've opened up a world for The Islanders series—and us. You are a brilliant connector and have a knack for understanding the heart of our message. We are so fortunate to have you on our team. Thank you!

Pat Denkler, whose passion for wildlife and connections with organizations that protect habitat, has brought our books to the attention of a wider audience. Thank you!

Molly Waring, Ballyhoo & Co., your sense of style, wordsmith talents, and your heart for Charleston are a joy and a blessing. We love our website!

On Dewees Island, great love and thanks to:

Judy Drew Fairchild, whose passion for nature is inspiring and whose patience with our questions is unending, we are beyond grateful. Your stories, photos, and nature notes are magic. (If you love Dewees and the nature depicted in The Islanders series, be sure to follow Nature Walks with Judy on social media. Teachers, it is a great resource, too.) We extend our gratitude to your husband, Reggie, as well as Ted, Kate, and Emily, who all share your love for the wild. You are also an amazing copy editor!

Alicia Reilly, whose love for Dewees and gift for storytelling kept us inspired and enthralled. We especially thank Ian and Cold for taking us out to the creeks and sharing with us the stories of middle-grade boys who live a Huck Finn life on the island. Priceless!

Claudia Poulnot de Mayo, for sharing your gorgeous photography, which keeps us connected to the island, and for allowing us to share your home as a base to do research and be inspired.

Carey Sullivan, for working so hard with Judy on the Dewees Island Nature Center and the incredible mural, which was serendipitous timing with the writing of this book.

Brucie and Low, you always have the light shining for us to share friends, stories, and good times.

The Dewees Island community, for their commitment to protecting their wild island and all its inhabitants and being a positive example to communities everywhere that you can live in harmony with the wild. Thank you for embracing The Islanders series, and us. We are eternally grateful.

Laura Caudill, Abby Wiseman, and Meghan Teumer, the Dewees Island Interns, for your knowledge, stories, and an introduction to Pierre.

We are also deeply grateful to:

Sally Murphy. Once more we are indebted to my mentor and dear friend. You are not only renowned for your work with SCDNR and sea turtles (which you wrote about so beautifully in your memoir, *Turning the Tide*), but we are grateful for your eagle-eyed copy editing. We devoured your notes and the manuscript is better—and more accurate—for them. Thank you for your expertise, your great stories, and of course, your friendship.

Nic Butler, PhD Historian, Charleston County Public Library, for your enthusiastic help sharing your knowledge and ideas with us about treasures in the Lowcountry.

Jason Roberts, retired USMC, for sharing some of your personal experience as a war veteran and amputee.

And last, we thank those who come first in our lives: our husbands, children, and grandchildren, who are patient, under-standing, and supportive of our writing careers. None of this could be possible without the love of our families.

ABOUT THE AUTHORS

MARY ALICE MONROE is the *New York Times* bestselling author of twenty-seven books, including the bestselling Beach House series. Monroe also writes children's picture books and a new middle-grade fiction series, The Islanders. Monroe is a member of the South Carolina Academy of Authors' Hall of Fame, and her books have received numerous awards, including the South Carolina Center for the Book Award for Writing, the South Carolina Award for Literary Excellence, the SW Florida Author of Distinction Award, the RT Lifetime Achievement Award, the International Book Award for Green Fiction, and the Henry Bergh Award for Children's Fiction, and her novel *A Lowcountry Christmas* won the prestigious Southern Prize for Fiction. *The Beach House* is a Hallmark Hall of Fame movie starring Andie McDowell. Several of her novels are optioned for film. She is the cocreator of the weekly web show and podcast Friends & Fiction. Monroe is also an active conservationist and serves on several boards. She lives on the South Carolina coast, which is a source of inspiration for many of her books.

ANGELA MAY is the founder of May Media and PR and a former award-winning television news journalist who helps promote great books and share important community stories as a media specialist. She has been working with Mary Alice Monroe for more than a decade. *The Islanders* was their first book together! Angela's husband is a middle school assistant principal. They have two children and live in Mount Pleasant, South Carolina. Connect with her at angelamaybooks.com.